Ecstasy
in Red

LYNNE
CONNOLLY

ELLORA'S CAVE
ROMANTICA®
www.EllorasCave.com

An Ellora's Cave Publication

www.ellorascave.com

Red Shadow

ISBN 9781419965838
ALL RIGHTS RESERVED.
Red Shadow Copyright © 2009 Lynne Connolly
Edited by Briana St. James.
Cover art by Syneca.

Electronic book publication December 2009
Trade paperback publication 2012

RED SHADOW

ဆ

Chapter One

ဢ

Johann turned his wrath on Jack Hargreaves as they stood in front of the monitors watching the guests arrive for the charity auction. "What do you mean you know her?" They watched the tall, elegant woman move across the screens from the imposing lobby of the Timothy hotel to the elevators that would take her up to the ballroom. She looked too perfect for sex.

Jack shrugged, his shoulders barely moving inside his elegant tuxedo jacket. "I had her earlier this year in New York. She's some kind of celebrity journalist. She was after some rough English trade, so I gave it to her."

Chase groaned. "When you were investigating that building for STORM." Dressed in a tuxedo like Jack's, he was the epitome of elegance, his blond hair shining in the harsh light of the security booth. The owner of the Timothy group, Chase was heading up this investigation into the whereabouts of rogue scientist Dr. Bennett. With any luck, Johann thought, they might finish this one before the fourth member of the team, Ricardo Gianetti, got here from Seattle. All they had to do was make the contact with their informant, who said she'd be here tonight, and then close the labs down and capture Bennett. He had hopes this would be an open and shut case and they'd all be on their way back to New York in a few days. He hoped so, anyway, because he hated LA. Too sunny for this vampire.

Jack chuckled. "That's the one. I was playing Jack the English plumber. She caught me digging around her boyfriend's apartment on Seventy-Sixth, so the best way to distract her was to take her to bed. I think I persuaded her all the pipes were in order." Jack's wolfish grin didn't appease Johann who knew what was coming next.

"Okay, guys, switch places." Chase exchanged a wry grin with Johann, his bright blue eyes failing to hide his amusement. He knew how much Johann loved fronting operations. Not at all.

Johann groaned. "Shit. Gimme the tux."

Johann heard Chase's chuckle echo through his head as he crossed the lobby of the hotel and climbed the stairs to the ballroom. He'd know that laugh anywhere, although he'd heard it more often recently. He tugged at the sleeves of Jack's tuxedo jacket to try to restore it to something similar to the tailor-made one he'd left at home.

You are one sick bastard, he informed Chase, using their secure telepathic link. *You should be here turning on the charm, not me.*

Jillian might kill me. Jillian adored Chase, as he adored her. Nice for them, but it meant Johann was stuck with this assignment, since newly married men didn't seduce other women, especially when they'd made it so obvious to anyone who cared how much in love they were. Didn't work. All they knew was that their contact was female, so they'd have to go in expecting romance or, at the very least, flirtation. Johann didn't do flirtation. He did sex.

This definitely should be Jack, who women unaccountably seemed to like. They wanted to mother him, not knowing the jaguar shape-shifter lurking under the human skin. Or perhaps they did know. These days everybody knew.

Johann would have snorted, but he was trying to appear suave. Hard enough in this damn tux. The best he could hope for was an in-and-out job. Make contact, find the lab's location and go.

Johann couldn't even remember the official excuse for this shindig. Some charity fundraiser or other, an auction and a ball. They should have just given their money to the charity, but then there wouldn't be that priceless opportunity to see and be seen. The auction had just taken place and people were making their way to the ballroom for the next part of the event. The all-important socializing part.

The lobby was filled with people wending their way upstairs but he deliberately chose to go alone.

Once he contacted the woman, he could leave and then help to track down and destroy another fucking laboratory, one of those hellholes where Talents had been tortured as part of a plan to extract their gifts and sell them. They were doomed to failure but it didn't stop them trying.

The thought of that didn't improve his mood. But his first sight on entering the ballroom did.

He waved away a drinks tray. The man holding it glanced at the blonde waitress holding a similar tray and grinned.

Small, blonde and cute. Johann liked her compact, curvy figure. Things were looking up. She wore a typical waitress's outfit, a neat black blouse and skirt, not too short, not too tight, with black hosiery that Johann found himself hoping were stockings rather than passion-killing pantyhose. Over it, she wore a crisp white apron, no frills. A parody would have had the apron surrounded by frills, the skirt flirty and tiny, showing glimpses of the stocking tops, maybe a corset-style top or no top at all, breasts contained in the apron. But that would have tilted sexy over to sleazy and sleazy had stopped interesting him a long time ago.

Johann tried to read her telepathically and couldn't. His telepathy wasn't his strongest gift even when, as now, he was in full possession of his vampire powers but her block suggested a natural barrier, one some mortals had almost from birth.

She got closer and so did the tingle in his mind. Sure, he enjoyed looking at the curvy, compact body but it wasn't the drinks she held that he wanted.

He glanced around and caught sight of a cool brunette dressed in a tight-fitting black knee-length dress that showed all her curves. Slim, elegant curves, matching the dark hair swept into a chignon. Her lips were glossed, her eyes shaded, but the whole effect was so perfect he found it a turn-off. He watched her as she set her sights on him and came closer. He scanned her mind. Ah. This one was the one from the labs. He could see the knowledge at the forefront of her mind. Maybe he'd have a chance to get to the blonde later.

She walked closer with a sassy sway of hip. Johann let the merest smidgeon of information out, felt her grab the knowledge of his Talent, saw her dark eyes sparkle.

"May I help you, sir?" Not a guest here then. He needed to get her alone, then they could capture her, Chase could strip her mind for the location of the labs and they could get the hell out of LA. He spared the blonde one last, regretful thought and turned his mind back to his job.

So he gave the brunette a smile and turned on the charisma, the glamour that drew prey to him and now drew her. Her eyes widened and she blinked, turning it into a flirtatious glance up at his face through her lashes. Johann smiled at her. "That depends. What do you have to offer?" He suppressed his wince. That was the worst line he'd ever heard, much less delivered.

But it worked. "Whatever you want." Her smile broadened. "My name's Jeanine. Jeanine McCray. I'm managing the catering tonight and I can promise you that all the girls here are at your service. We offer more than food." Her look smoldered with promise.

That would work. It would get her out of this ballroom to a place he could take her without making a fuss.

"We should discuss this later. Your room or mine?"

I'm in the ballroom, watching your six. Is she the link?

Johann didn't turn around. He knew Chase's cool, precise tones whether spoken or mind to mind. *Seems so.*

I sense other Talents in the room.

Not all Talents are out. Or even on our side.

True enough.

Chase was too trusting sometimes. But with a mortal lifespan he hadn't seen as much sick behavior as Johann had. Good to have him as a backup though. Chase had a cool temperament and a useful pair of hands. And feet, come to that. No one looking at the suave, sophisticated hotel owner would imagine that he could deliver a roundhouse kick they'd be proud of in the kickboxing ring. But Johann had seen it and been glad of it.

Waitstaff circulated with glasses of something that looked like champagne cocktails. He took one and pretended to take a sip. Vile stuff. It was well after sunset now and he'd be sick to his stomach if he drank any of it.

The brunette leaned closer and he got a whiff of her perfume. It smelled expensive and French. Everything about her was refined and cool. And controlled. "The girls here all perform a variety of functions. Take your pick and I'll arrange it for you."

Johann's stomach turned. This woman was into more than illegal Bennett lab activities. He did what he should have done at first, but all the coming out crap had made him warier of opening his powers in public. They might be out, but he preferred to keep a low profile. But he had to read her. So he opened his mind and entered hers.

What he read made him heartsick, that such corruption should fester in the heart of her. This woman would lead him straight to the mother lode. Although he didn't penetrate to her innermost thoughts, he didn't need to. She was disorganized inside and all her thoughts had one end — money. Dollars floated through her mind. In collusion with her boss, the absent Sheila, she acquired Talents for the labs for cash, she prostituted the girls who worked for her for cash. Maybe soon she could afford that beach house she had her eye on.

11

She'd never reach that beach house if Johann could help it. Once she'd led them to the lab, she was done.

Want me to break her? Chase was a powerful Sorcerer. He could fracture most minds without breaking into a sweat. Not that he did it very often. But if he did it to this woman he'd be doing a lot of other people a favor.

Let's get her out of here. Somewhere quieter. He leaned closer. "You do personal services? Get your own—hands—dirty?" He upped the charm factor.

She blinked, her heavily mascaraed lashes sweeping her cheeks. "It's not something I usually do."

He knew her weakness now. "Give me an hour of your time and I'll give you five thousand for it."

She licked her lips, already glistening with lip gloss. "I can't do it yet. I have to supervise this function." And get some more customers, he'd bet. "Later, I'll do whatever you want." She smiled. Not completely impervious to a little mental push then.

Johann ran his fingers down her bare lower arm and felt her shiver. "I'll look forward to it. Don't go far." He slipped a card to her, a keycard to the room where they'd take her. "The number's on the card. As soon as you can, say a couple of hours?"

She raised a brow and swept a glance over him. "Are you sure you can afford it? Extras are—extra."

Johann smiled. "You shouldn't always judge by appearances. This tux is a last-minute hire. Mine is somewhere between here and New York. I only got in today."

She relaxed. "Then I should be able to give you a hearty welcome to Los Angeles."

He sensed Chase's presence closer. *I'll chat to her. As the hotel owner, I can take an interest. Make her sweat a little bit.*

Are you sure that's wise?

Johann saw the gleam of bared teeth in his mind. Amazing how he could do that. *Trust me. I want to keep tabs on her and if you stick by her all evening people will notice. And I want to soften her up a little. When I go in, I don't want to kill her immediately.*

That made sense. Chase could penetrate to the back of someone's mind instantly but if he did it without warning, he could kill them. Getting close to her meant he could sense her patterns, find weak spots and use them instead. They didn't want her dead. Or rather, STORM didn't. Johann wouldn't extend that to himself. Dead would suit him fine.

"Is everything all right here?" Chase's urbane voice cut into the flirting. He'd never been so glad to see his colleague before, even when Chase was saving his neck or he was saving Chase's.

"Perfect." Johann glanced at him. "I was just complimenting Jeanine here on the service this evening. The waitstaff are working well."

Chase addressed Jeanine directly. "I'm pleased so far. We use our own people normally, but we were pushed tonight with two other functions, so I decided to give your company a try. So far I'm impressed. Can you tell Ms. Zelinski I'll call her in the morning?"

Now it was Chase's turn to receive the blinding smile. "I haven't met her yet. Her partner employed me, but she's away on leave right now. I'll be delighted to pass on your message in the morning."

Johann's cue to leave. He'd pick her up later. He nodded to her and smiled.

Then two things happened. The orchestra struck up for the first waltz. And a crash made him jump out of his skin. The little blonde waitress had finally reached him and dropped her tray.

Chapter Two

ഇ

Ania trembled in reactive shock, staring at the pieces of shattered glass. The wine had splashed up over her legs and the lower part of her skirt. She'd been watching the tall, dark stranger so avidly she'd almost missed the presence of Chase Maynord. The only person in the place who'd recognize her.

Ania tried to back off when she saw him with her boss for tonight, but Jeanine had seen her and her mouth thinned. She knew why. Ania was here as a substitute for one of Jeanine's regulars, a woman called Virginia, and if ever there was an inappropriate name, that was it, because as soon as she'd arrived Jeanine had clued her in to her little scam.

After hours, Jeanine ran an "introduction service", for commission. None of which found its way back to Simply Service, the company she co-owned with Sheila Murtagh. The caterers employed here tonight. At the Timothy, one of the flagship LA hotels. Ania wanted to howl in frustration. Sheila had stitched her up good. A year she'd had away from work, and look what had happened.

Sheila was as upper class as Ania wasn't, so they'd made a good partnership right from the start, or at least Ania had thought so. Until Sheila suddenly left town just after Ania returned to work and started to uncover some unpleasant facts. Like Sheila had been siphoning money off the company for some time. Like some of the payments into the company had come from sources that, when Ania had checked, had proved to be bogus, payments she doubted had any legitimate origin. Mailboxes and companies that were mere fronts. Like this meant she was on the brink of bankruptcy.

She was beyond mad, way, way beyond pissed. This meant that a couple of hundred staff plus casuals would lose their jobs. Worse, if Sheila and Jeanine really had been using her company as a front for prostitution and God knew what else, she could be subject to prosecution.

She needed proof. Everything was carefully covered up, so she couldn't get a paper trail. She'd see it for herself and then she'd call in the cops before they called on her. It was her only chance.

So she came here tonight because she knew no one on duty. This was Jeanine's team, the one Sheila wanted to nurture for "special events". How special Ania hadn't realized, but she knew now.

The waitstaff here were dressed in the uniform, simple black skirt or pants with a shirt bearing the Simply Service logo — a little waiter in red — and a white apron for the women. Only the skirts were too short and tight, the aprons see-through and skimpy. Special services her ass.

She was so mad she could hardly think, but she'd forced herself into calmness, listened when, at the beginning of the evening, Jeanine had explained, tactfully and carefully, what "special services" actually meant. Nothing definite, just thirty percent for an introduction and a further forty percent of any "extra" fees earned. Once she saw the guys working tonight, she saw them for what they were — a mixture of gigolos and pure muscle.

Chase Maynord would see through this in a snap. She couldn't stop what had happened tonight, but she could run interference. Trouble was, if Maynord saw her here, he might assume she was involved. She'd attempted a bit of disguise, applied heavy makeup and done her hair differently, the best she could do at short notice, but nobody recognized her. Not until she'd seen Maynord.

Which was why she was here, posing as casual labor for her own company, trying desperately to get some evidence she could give the cops, plus evidence that she wasn't involved.

That was an outside chance but it was all she had to play for right now. The only chance she had of saving her business and her good name. To sell out her partner.

It sucked. The whole thing sucked big hairy ones. But Sheila deserved it and Ania wouldn't go down for something somebody else had done.

She hadn't been prepared to see the most gorgeous man she'd ever set eyes on in her life. The high, slanted cheekbones, the dark hair, cut sleekly to follow the lines of his perfectly rounded skull, the clean, crisp lines of his body, hinting at a powerful frame underneath. Everything called to her, something deep inside, something she hadn't felt for years, and when he turned and his dark gaze had skimmed over her she'd melted like a sophomore in front of the new English professor.

She hated herself for it. She had enough to do without this.

He had a word with Jeanine, and she knew from the way he touched her, so lightly, and the way she leaned her head closer to him that Jeanine was setting him up with someone. This might be her proof. She knew he'd seen her. She could get in on this. So she moved closer.

Then she'd seen Chase Maynord and her little plan had all gone to shit. She had no choice. She dropped the tray. And followed it down soon after, babbling about clearing it up. Her fine hair had already mostly fallen out of the chignon she'd put it in and she let more come loose to cover her face.

"Hey, be careful, there's broken glass everywhere."

Shocked, she moved her hand and felt the sting. Crying out, she pulled away and felt the glass scratch her hand. "Oh no!" Instinctive reaction had her bringing her hand to her mouth, sucking the side where the glass had touched.

A strong hand pulled it away. "Let me see."

Silence surrounded them like their own island of peace. A touch, warm and strong, took her hand in a warm grasp. A male rumble of sympathy.

She knew who had her hand, who had hunkered down to help her. Tall, dark and oomph. She tried to think rationally. This man could save her from Chase recognizing her and assuming she was in on the deal. But all she could feel was his hand, warm against hers, and the slightly rough texture of his handkerchief when he pressed it against her wound. His touch shot through her senses. He drew it away and then replaced it after he'd folded it to a clean side. "It's not so bad. You won't need stitches."

"Are you sure?" She had to get out of here before Maynord recognized her and blew her cover. "I think there's a first aid guy downstairs. Maybe I should go see him."

"I've done some first aid. Enough to know you're breathing regularly, not unconscious and not bleeding to death. Look, let's get out of here so I can treat it for you."

That suited her perfectly.

She let her hair fall over her face, but just before she exited the ballroom, someone stood in her way. Jeanine. A quick glance showed her Chase was standing a little way off. She pivoted so he couldn't see her face.

"I hope you realize that you needn't bother coming back?"

She met Jeanine's gaze and bit her lower lip, the best she could do right now to offer regret. But a tutting sound reminded her she wasn't alone. "Could you please move aside? This woman is bleeding."

Jeanine spared a glance at Ania's napkin-shrouded hand. She sniffed. "We can't have blood on the glasses. Perhaps it's as well they were smashed. Normally I'd expect you to clear up the mess, but I suppose you'll have to take care of your hand first. I'll get someone else to deal with it. I'm most displeased." She glanced at the man beside her. "You don't have to concern yourself with this, sir. I'm so sorry about it. Since the band has just struck up, may I introduce you to a suitable partner?" She moved aside to stand in front of Chase Maynord, effectively blocking his view.

The man smiled. "I have some first aid experience and the accident was more than half my fault. I wish you would reconsider your decision to fire her."

Jeanine's smile was all about sex and nothing about sincerity. "I have to stand by my decision." She paused. "Unless you would prefer to engage her services."

Ania caught her breath. How dare this woman be so blatant? She had to get out of this fast, before Jeanine implicated her. Her heart plummeted.

Her expression must have fooled Jeanine into thinking she was in despair, because the woman put up her elegant, pointed chin and stared down her nose at her. She must have four inches advantage on Ania, especially since Ania had dumped her usual high heels in favor of flats tonight. Jeanine hadn't, which would make her around five ten in stockinged feet.

It didn't help to know that.

Elegant, classy women had always intimidated her. She couldn't help what she was or that underneath lay a bullied schoolgirl who'd never quite lost her awe of the soignée seniors, but at least she'd gotten better at hiding it.

This time she didn't try. She let her hair hang over her face and bowed her head. "I only dropped a tray."

"I'll have the bill for damages sent on to you."

Then the stranger next to her surprised her. He reached into his pocket and drew out a wallet before handing Ania a couple of bills. Two hundred bucks. "If that doesn't cover it, let me know. I was at least half to blame." Before she could protest, which she had every intention of doing, he cupped her elbow and gave her a gentle push. "We really have to get that cut seen to. Can't have you bleeding all over the ballroom." He guided her out, but not before he leaned toward Jeanine and murmured, "I'll see you later. Don't forget."

"No, of course not," she replied, but they were already on their way.

They stepped into an elevator and he pushed a button, then pushed her elbow so her hand was thrust up. "Hold it up until we get there."

"Where?"

"My suite."

He said nothing until they were out of the elevator and partway along one of the plush carpeted hallways that led to the hotel's suites. Not a room. She chuckled low in her throat, the sound escaping before she could suppress it. "The tux really was misleading."

With a lithe movement he pivoted to face her. She found his lopsided grin endearing. "Guess it was. Come on." He led her halfway down then swiped a card through a slot. What surprised her was the extra level of security when he pressed his thumb against a plate on the door.

She walked in after him. "That's not usual in hotels."

The large room was lit by soft lights inset in the ceiling and several table lamps, two of which he flipped on when he walked across to the large windows. "Come into the bathroom," he said.

Ania didn't think about not doing it until he led her past the large, Spanish-style bed to the well-appointed bathroom. She'd never seen a hotel room like it. Oh she knew they existed, but this was something else. Seeing it, smelling the delicately perfumed air, feeling the soft carpeting under her feet, added to the sense of luxury.

"Sit." The bathroom even had a chair. She was used to sitting on the toilet seat at home and she didn't exactly live in squalor. Obediently she sat on the soft cushions covering the cane seat. He shrugged off the coat and threw it over the back of the chair. "Let's see."

"It's not so bad." It stung, but it wasn't throbbing. She peeled off the napkin and revealed the cut.

He turned on the faucet over the sink and took the napkin from her, soaking the part that she'd left unstained. "I know. We'll clean it up and get a bandage on it. You should be fine."

He sounded completely unconcerned, totally unlike his attitude downstairs. As if he read her, he squatted down in front of her, taking her hand and turning it. He dabbed at the wound, wiping away the blood that made it look worse than it actually was. Ania shuddered. He paused and looked up at her. "Are you okay?"

It was worse when he looked at her, his dark eyes perceptive. Touch and sight. Now all she needed was taste. His voice was dark and velvety, his scent perfect, all soap and aftershave and pure male. And she knew she couldn't deny her attraction. The more she pretended it wasn't there, the worse it got and it had done so ever since she'd first met his gaze in the ballroom.

Warmth spread through her mind, as if, as if…

Shit.

His smile broadened. "Yes. I wondered if you'd notice before I told you." He examined her scratch, because that was all it was once he'd cleaned off the blood. "I'm a Talent."

She snatched her hand back but his hold on her wrist firmed and she found herself trapped. "Why didn't you say something before?" She tried to keep her breathing steady. She'd never knowingly been this close to a Talent before. Mythical creatures who'd been living among them all this time, vampires, shape-shifters, even merpeople. In the last year she'd seen a dragon on TV and a vampire talking calmly about his lifestyle on Larry King. And now she was staring at one. Her tension racked up to panic.

"Hey, calm down. We're human, just like you. Just a different kind of human."

Ania stared at the man, trying to imagine him as a different creature, changing his shape. But she couldn't see anything other than his broad-shouldered frame. "So you say."

He smiled. She wished he wouldn't do that. "You know I'm in the outer part of your mind, don't you? I read you when you dropped the tray. You didn't want Chase to recognize you. You two got history?"

She bit her lip. "Something like that." She didn't trust him enough to tell him the whole truth, at least not yet. After all, she'd heard Johann arrange to meet the hag later.

"Well, he's not available now. Jillian came back."

She frowned. "Jillian?"

He tilted his head to one side. "An old flame. The love of his life. He thought she'd died three years ago. She hadn't. So Chase is now a blissfully married man." His smile twisted to one of cynicism. "Sooner him than me."

"You don't believe in marriage?"

"I think it's fine—for other people." He touched the napkin to the wound then threw it aside. "That should do. Let's get this bandage on."

He crossed the room, something that would take him a maximum of two steps in her small bathroom, but in this room it took five strides. She counted. He opened a cabinet and took out a small pack of bandages, selecting a couple after rejecting one or two others. Fastidious then. Fussy, even.

"Very particular," he said as he came back to her.

"I wish you wouldn't do that," she said, irritated.

He looked up at her through his ridiculously thick lashes. "What?"

"Answer things I haven't asked, only thought."

"You should learn to control your thoughts."

"Yeah, right."

21

He carefully applied a bandage across one end of the long scratch. "That will sting for a couple of days." He took the other one and peeled off the backing tape. She coughed.

She stared at him and watched fire spark in his eyes. Perhaps he was a dragon. She'd love to see a dragon for real.

He bent down and presented his hand, his mouth quirking up in a smile. "I'm Johann Kozac. Pleased to meet you."

She took his hand in her unmarked right one. "Ania Zelinski."

"Polish?"

"Third generation. My grandparents came over in World War Two."

"I was Czech, came over at about the same time as your grandparents, I guess."

She stared at him. "I thought you were in your mid thirties. I guess it's hard to—to—"

"You're doing real well." His voice softened and he reached up a hand to smooth back her wayward hair. "Is this your first close encounter with a Talent?"

"I guess."

"Does it bother you?"

She gave a short laugh. "I used to read a lot of fairy stories when I was a kid. So when we heard Talents did exist, it was kinda expected. I don't know, but it didn't come as much of a surprise as it should have done. And now we know for sure."

"Come on." He tugged her to her feet. "Let's get a drink."

"Shouldn't you go back to the ball?" She let him draw her up and found herself disturbingly close to him. Close enough to feel the heat of his body against hers.

Instead of releasing her, he curved an arm around her waist. "My work there is done." He stroked her waist and she felt him through her clothes as if she were naked. Disturbingly intimate. "I'll gladly miss the rest of it."

She stayed where she was, staring up at him. His dark eyes filled with amusement—and something more. She didn't know if her tongue still worked and if she tried she was pretty sure she'd say something unbelievably stupid.

He drew a deep breath but didn't take his gaze away from her. "You are purely gorgeous, Ania Zelinski." He stared at her, his eyes sharp with realization. "Zelinski?"

Her shoulders sagged, the cheap, rough fabric of her blouse rasping against her shoulders. Some spy she made. "Yes, that's right. I'm one of the owners of Simply Service. The other one has left town. Bolted. I took a year off to—to deal with personal problems, and when I came back, I found this. I was supposed to ease back into work, but instead I found Sheila gone, the books in a mess and some weird references to escorts and services." She looked up at him. His dark eyes held stillness and alertness. At least he was listening. "I can't prove I'm not involved and I think Sheila fixed it that way, so she had somebody to take the fall. I was here tonight to find out more. This is Jeanine's team, and Sheila employed her and her people after I left so I thought nobody would know me. But I negotiated the original contract with Chase Maynord."

"He's furious."

"I don't blame him. So am I."

He spread his hand and placed it over her temple. "Let me read you."

"What, like the Vulcan mind meld?"

He smiled and it sent shivers right through her. It wasn't fair that she found him so attractive. Her nipples didn't know he could turn her in, her pussy, busy dampening her panties, couldn't understand her trepidation, only fed off the adrenaline he evoked and got itself ready for him. Insane, she had to be insane. "Nothing like it. I'm touching you because I enjoy it. Your hair is so silky it invites touch." He stroked her, making her want to purr like a cat. "I just want to touch your mind, read it a little deeper. Chase will probably want to do it for himself but I can usually tell a lie and so far I don't feel any."

He bit his lip as if thinking what to tell her. "I'm a friend of Chase's and he had his doubts about Simply Service so he asked me to help him. I've lured Jeanine in and made an appointment to meet her. In a couple of hours we'll have our answers."

She breathed out in relief. At least he believed she wasn't here to take part. She pulled away, realizing what he might assume from her reaction to him. His hot breath washed over her face, raising all kinds of thoughts she was quick to suppress. But not fast enough, it seemed, because he bent his head and touched his lips to hers.

Before she could lose herself completely in him, she pulled back, staring up into his now passion-drenched eyes. "But *I'm* not a prostitute."

"Good. I'm not looking for one." His eyelids drooped over those mesmerizing eyes and he leaned toward her again.

This time she didn't pull back. Their mouths met and it shocked her to her core how it felt so right and yet thrilled her completely with its newness. She'd never felt the same way before, never wanted a simple kiss so much. She had no time to explore the dichotomy and she wasn't sure she wanted to. All she knew was that it was pure magic.

Although the kiss was exploratory, it was anything but tentative. She shivered at the first contact and he responded, tightening his hold on her and opening his mouth to touch her lips with his tongue. All her senses went on alert. He smelled delicious, citrusy and musky at the same time, he must have shaved recently, because where his skin touched hers it caressed her with conditioned smoothness and his hands, firm on her body, didn't stray but the warmth seeped right through as if she were naked.

She heard his voice in his mind and it was simply the sexiest thing she'd ever experienced in her life. *Open for me, miláčku. Let me in.*

She couldn't have resisted if a pack of dogs was baying at her heels. She parted her lips and he surged inside.

It was as if a series of explosions went off in her head. The kind of explosions signaling a firework display, showers of bright sparks shimmered across her closed eyelids. This man was dangerous. Especially to her.

Or maybe to all women. Ania moved closer, aching to feel him, and lifted one leg, drawing it down his calf from his knee to his ankle. He growled into her mouth.

Oh yeah.

Fuck, was she in trouble.

Chapter Three

෨

He explored her mouth languorously and stroked his tongue against hers. Time stilled as she experienced and returned his caresses. She slid her hands around his waist to steady herself, feeling the bandage catch on his shirt then move on. The scratch didn't even sting anymore.

He drew away and she gave herself a moment before she opened her eyes. He didn't let her go when she tried to pull back, but loosened his hold a little. He gazed down at her, his eyes glazed. "Before you leave here, I want to build a mental barrier for you. Your thoughts are too open."

She started, hoping he hadn't noticed the secrets she'd been at great pains to conceal. He smiled. "You have certain areas I can't enter without hurting you, but you're spending too much effort maintaining them all. One big barrier, like a brick wall with a door in it, would be much more efficient." He touched his lips to her frown. "That's not the only thing I want to do, but that, my lovely girl, is up to you."

Thoughts raced through her head, made worse by her inability to conceal them. "Will you promise to stay out of my mind unless I invite you in?"

Slowly, he nodded. "If that's what you want. Although I'll have to enter to build your barrier. Once I've done it you can maintain it. I'll ask first, I promise." He lifted a hand and stroked it over her forehead. "You have beautiful skin. Like porcelain."

"It's genetic. My mother has—had it too."

He was giving her time to think. She knew and appreciated it, but his patience wasn't endless. His eyes sparkled with little red lights and his body, taut against hers, throbbed with anticipation.

Every reason she thought of she dismissed—a one-night stand, her first. So what? Maybe it was about time. Health reasons—she was clean and she knew Talents didn't get diseases. She couldn't think of a single reason not to.

She looked up at him and smiled. "Yes." And then the reasons why she should flooded her mind but the only important one was that she thought he was the hottest thing she'd seen in years. And he wanted her.

He didn't give her a chance to change her mind but took her mouth again, this time plundering her. She plundered back, opening her mouth wide to take him and shoving her hands under his shirt to touch bare skin.

The contact sizzled through her and she felt him flinch, but he didn't pull away. He gasped into her mouth. She expected the flavor of alcohol because the attendees had been plied with drink since their arrival; something more than one of them had commented on and laughed at. But this man tasted of pure male. She hadn't even known what that tasted like before.

He pulled away and she heard his breath in the sudden silence, coming shorter than before. He pulled the ties of her apron loose and lifted it over her head, shifting just enough to give it room to fall to the floor. Then he started on the buttons of her blouse.

Panic hit her. Had she worn the old bra, the comfortable one that had gone gray with washing? Oh God, she had. That sucked.

But she needn't have worried because he hardly looked. He reached around her, flicked the clasp open and drew the cups down over her breasts. Then he looked. He stared for what seemed like forever and together they watched her nipples harden into tight peaks. "What a gorgeous sight."

Well if he didn't mention her bra, she wouldn't. Besides, he was touching her now. She'd keep that bra forever, as a souvenir and a reminder of how his hands felt on her skin.

After one gentle stroke to each breast with the backs of his fingers, he tugged her blouse clear of her skirt and skimmed it down her arms. She shook it off and brought her arms forward to get rid of the bra. Only just in time, as he dragged her back to him. "I was right. You're stunning."

Although Ania didn't have the skinny looks of a top model, she'd never had complaints. But all her previous encounters paled next to this. They'd been fun, sharing times for the most part, with a mistake or two along the way. Six to be precise, with one long-term relationship. All in the past.

Just one touch from Johann blew them all out of the water. He gave her a slow smile and reached for her skirt zipper. "Is this something Talents do?" she managed.

"What's that, *miláčku?*"

"Wh-what you're doing now?"

He glanced down at his hands, busy with the button at the top of her skirt. "Isn't this the way it's usually done?"

She managed a tremulous smile in response to his. "Never mind. This is just a bit—intense."

"Yeah." His voice deepened, roughened. "Me too. And no, it's nothing to do with me being anything other than a man. Just forget everything else."

Her skirt slid down her legs and he groaned. "I knew it. Stockings. Oh baby."

All Ania could think was that she was glad she'd worn a pair of black panties to match the only garter belt she possessed. She hated pantyhose, usually went bare-legged or wore socks. The strip of flesh at the top of her thighs gleamed in the low light. She could smell her arousal now, her musk blending with his. And he was still fully dressed, except that she'd untucked his shirt.

And then he wasn't so dressed anymore. He ripped away his bow tie and tore at his shirt, not bothering to slide the buttons through the holes as he'd done with her. Buttons burst over them, then fell to the floor, disregarded. "I just want to feel those pretty nipples against my skin," he muttered and dragged her close. They both gasped at the contact. His hot, hard chest burned into her as her breasts cuddled against him, then squashed. His mouth came down on hers in raw possession. He owned her now. What she didn't know was if she owned him in return.

Right now she didn't care. His tongue plunged deep and then withdrew. He pressed kisses to the side of her mouth and down her neck, her pulse leaping to meet his tongue as he flicked it over the base of her throat. His growl reverberated against her skin and she threw back her head to give him as much access as he needed. He licked, sucked and played at the sensitive skin before he moved to her shoulder, then her breast.

She gave a sharp cry and clutched his head, threading her fingers through his hair, teasing it out of the sleek style he'd put it in. Almost black, rain-straight and soft, it caressed her hands as his tongue was caressing her breasts. He placed precise, tiny kisses around her nipple before he sucked it gently into his mouth. She wanted hard.

His hands curved around her thighs, shaping them, massaging through her stockings and then he cupped her buttocks. Ania nearly lost her balance then. She could do nothing but feel.

He kissed her flesh, nuzzling, slight prickles revealing that he'd shaved in a hurry and missed a couple of bristles. It only added to the heightened sensations she couldn't control anymore.

He lifted her and swung her into his arms, the maneuver seemingly effortless. She knew Talents had incredible strength, but now she felt it and the two were entirely different experiences. Curling close to his chest, she felt deliciously feminine and helpless, two things she rarely allowed herself to experience these days. He smiled down at her and paused for a kiss, gentle but filled with passion, before he laid her on the bed and stood back to look at her. "Take off your panties," he said.

The words made her shudder and she knew this was the ultimate acceptance of him. Once that flimsy piece of material was gone, she would be accepting him and that dark promise in his eyes.

She slid her panties off her hips and sat up to pull them off the rest of the way but when she brought her hands up to her garter belt to unhook the stockings, he stopped her. "Leave them. I like the way they frame you."

Ania flushed, the hot blood flooding her skin, and he groaned, then smiled at her, his eyes gleaming with desire. His hands went to his thin black belt, then the button on his pants and he stripped without looking at anything but her. Greatly daring, she opened her legs a little wider.

His lids dropped across his eyes as he swept her body with his gaze and she felt the goose bumps rise with it. No man had ever stopped and looked at her like that before and she liked it. And it gave her a chance to look at him too.

Dark hair sprinkled his powerful chest, taut muscle delineating it like a charcoal sketch. Lightly tanned skin led to a paler area below the waist, but not too pale, suggesting that sometimes, at least, he faced the sun naked.

And he was erect, the dark head straining toward her as if it would take her on its own. She loved that. As she watched, a few drops of liquid escaped from the top. Without taking his gaze off her, he reached down and grasped it, pushing the skin up, and only then did she realize he was uncircumcised. As far as she was concerned that just gave her more to play with. It would be a sin to mutilate that beautiful cock.

A slow smile gave him to-die-for creases between his nose and mouth. "Do I use protection?" he asked. A wary expression crossed his face, putting a shield in his eyes, and then was gone, as if he'd purposely dispelled it.

"Is there any reason to use it?" She had to be sure.

"To make you comfortable. That's all."

What the hell, she'd go with it. "Then there isn't any reason." She wet her lips and he closed his eyes. When he opened them again she would have sworn they burned her.

He put one knee on the bed and slid his body over so it took all his weight. Still he didn't touch her, although he was only an inch away from her leg. Then he placed one hand on the far side of her before easing over her. Heat radiated off him and she lay still while he straddled her body and stared down at her. Slowly, he bent his head until his lips were a fraction away from hers. Then he paused. "Don't close your eyes," he murmured and kissed her.

It felt like she'd waited forever for that kiss. When his body lowered slowly on hers she sighed into his mouth and, without warning, his kiss turned savage. He opened his lips over hers and licked the roof of her mouth, sending her whirling into a world of sensation. Despite what he'd told her, her eyelids fluttered closed and immediately he pulled away. "Open them."

She blinked. "Is this some kind of Talent thing?"

"No. It's a Johann thing." He smiled against her mouth. "I love to watch eyes, especially yours. You've denied me your mind but you have the most beautiful eyes. Clear blue, like a robin's egg."

She caught her breath on a laugh. "You can't make me laugh at a time like this."

"Why not?" His voice turned so gentle now, she couldn't believe he was the same man whose cock was leaving damp kisses on her stomach, pushing against her with an insistence that turned her to jelly. "You should laugh. Sex is a joyful thing, done right."

"And do you do it right?"

His smile reached into the depths of his eyes. So close, she could see the dark rings around the chestnut centers, with the reddish sparks she'd noticed earlier. "That's for you to say."

He lifted and slid his cock between her thighs. It touched her, glided between her labia, over her clit, and without thinking she moved back, rubbed against it in an instinctive motion that sent shivers up her spine.

Another kiss, this one brief, then he drew back and took hold of his shaft, guiding it to where they both wanted it to be. He nudged her pussy, now yawning wide for him, and she caught her breath as the tip slid inside. He pushed the flanged head past the initial resistance but it still wasn't easy. They watched each other.

"Am I supposed to say it's not going to fit?" she said, knowing it would, but it might take a little work first.

He laughed and his cock slipped in even farther. "See what I mean about laughing? It's good for you."

Without warning he thrust hard and she felt his balls meet the lower curve of her ass. Her knees went up and she put her feet flat on the bed and pushed up, her back arching as she strained to meet him. And still they watched each other.

The black pupils expanded, covering half the golden brown. She gripped his shoulders but he pulled his upper body away from her, staring down at her. He held his weight on one hand as he cupped her breast, stroked the nipple and added to the incredible sensations coursing through her body. "Sweetheart, you are beautiful. With that hair, those wonderful blue eyes, I don't have to enter your mind. You're just as expressive without it."

She strained up. She wanted hard, fast, *now*. "Johann, please..."

"Oh yes." He put his hand back and lifted out of her, only to slam back inside. She howled when he collided with her sweet spot deep inside. She arched to bring it into contact with him and he lifted and thrust. Perfect.

Shudders spread through her as he worked her, harder, nearer and she felt him deep inside. When he lifted again, she felt his fingers between her labia, opening her up, and he came back down to her. This time his cock rubbed her clit with every stroke.

He stopped and she immediately hooked her legs around his waist, afraid he'd leave her. Not now, for God's sake, not now! "Don't stop." She tried to pull him back inside her but he resisted. Too easily.

"Open your eyes, Ania. Look at me."

She hadn't realized she'd closed them. She opened them to see his, the gold brown of his pupils almost gone, red, like sparkling rubies, holding all the rim. Was he a dragon? All shape-shifters were what people used to think of as mythical beasts. Only they weren't mythical, just hiding. A griffin? Maybe a wyvern? The notion thrilled her, but not as much as this man, here and now.

"You're thinking too much. Just feel. And don't close your eyes again."

She wouldn't. Not if he stopped when she did it. But when he drove deep inside her again, the sensations returned, and although it took two or three strokes to get her to the state she'd been in when he paused, she relished every thrust and began to wonder if the frustration wasn't worth it when her breath caught on a wave of heat.

It started deep inside her and spread to every part of her, then pulsed. She twisted against him, the sensation almost too much for her, but he held her firm, coming back down to press his hips against hers, holding her steady while he took her mouth in a deep, frantic kiss.

Still she kept her eyes open, afraid he'd make good on his promise to stop. She'd die if he did that now.

Her orgasm came in deep hard throbs, definite and separate, so she could have counted them if she wasn't going out of her mind from the waves coursing through her whole body. She arched up, sobbed her release and at the last moment he varied his rhythm, pulling out and driving back in halfway with short, sharp jabs that pushed her clit into exploding sensation.

Shuddering, fighting him for control of her own body, she realized she was crying his name. And then he was crying hers and he came on the heels of her climax. She felt the pulses within her as his seed jetted deep.

Sweat broke out on his body and on hers and he fell forward, then rolled, but didn't let her go.

She opened her eyes. He lifted a hand and stroked the side of her face. "Not very good at following instructions, are you?" But he smiled as he said it.

"I try to be, but I don't think I am." She snuggled in, loving the feel of his hot, large body. It enclosed her, made her feel safe and secure. Neither of which she was used to feeling. Since the age of eighteen she'd made her own safety and security, never trusting anyone else to do it, even though she'd been surrounded by people only too glad to take control. She just didn't trust anyone enough. But this man whom she'd known barely an hour, she would trust with her life.

She couldn't understand it, but she didn't really care right now.

He pressed a soft kiss to her forehead. "Hey."

She kissed his chin. "Hey yourself." And smiled. "Nobody's ever done that to me before."

"What's that?"

"Given me a vaginal orgasm and a clitoral one almost at the same time. You are amazing."

He chuckled. "Thank you, ma'am. I live to please." He drew back a little and his gaze intensified. "It was a decided pleasure. And I definitely want to do it again."

"You do?" The thought of continuing past this night struck her as a little scary. He'd obviously recovered his senses earlier than she had, because she was still too far gone enjoying the sensations he'd just gifted her with.

"Oh yeah. Do you think missionary is the only way I want you or we can explore all the possibilities in one night? You're delicious, Ania. You have a delectable body and a gift for staying in the present."

She slid her hand across his chest, just because she could. "That's not like me. I'm usually thinking about the next job or exams or hospitals." She bit her lip. She wasn't ready to let out too much about her life. Not yet. She wanted to regain control of it first. At the moment it sucked and all she wanted to do was forget it for a while.

He didn't follow up her slip about hospitals. Most likely he hadn't heard her because he was busy nuzzling her neck in a very distracting way.

She touched his hair again. It fascinated her, its thickness, the blue-black color, its silky texture. "Are you in LA for long?"

He lifted his head. "You've given me a reason to stay." He propped himself on one elbow and reached across to settle his hand over her waist. He spread his fingers wide and stroked her. "I hate this place. Always have. Nobody walks and there's no center. It's like no other place I know."

"I know. I guess I'm used to it. I was born not so far away and it was always the city to us. Even if I use far too much sunscreen. I keep my local drugstore in business with all the sunblock I buy."

He traced an imaginary line across her stomach. "I did notice you don't have the obligatory tan."

"It's the visitors who have the tan. When you live here, you try not to. It's not good for you."

"I know. And your skin is so delicate. Maybe you should think about moving somewhere with a little less sun."

She laughed. "My life is here." Then she stopped. The way things were going she'd have nothing soon. Unless she did some serious damage control. But that was nothing to do with her presence here and now. This was to make her feel better and he had seriously succeeded. Maybe she might think of moving on. No, not in these circumstances. She never ran away and she wasn't about to start now. She'd done nothing wrong, she just had to hold on and see what she could do to save herself and her company.

Enough for now. This man had promised not to enter her mind but he was a Talent and he might pick up things without meaning to. "What's it like living for a long time, going from life to life, trying to blend in? And what's it like now that you don't have to anymore?"

"Are you a journalist?" He gave a sudden grin. "You could be. To answer your question, in case you wanted an honest answer, moving from life to life was reality for me, normal. And now, I don't know how to handle it, but it's a relief not to have to do it anymore. That do?"

She smiled. "I'm not a journalist. Just naturally curious."

"Anything else you're curious about?" He took her hand and put it on his stomach, easing it down.

Her eyes widened when she felt the beginning of a fresh erection. "Is this something else Talents do?"

"Only when they find an irresistible woman." He caught his breath on a gasp when she stroked over the emerging head. "Oh yeah. Just keep doing that."

So she did. It worked and she loved the way his cock hardened under her touch. It gave her a sense of power, the way he lay back and just—let her, watching her all the time. But she felt no intrusion into her mind.

Suddenly he laughed and she stopped stroking him. "Is this ticklish?"

"No." He cupped her head and brought her closer. "Chase just contacted me. Wanted to know what I was doing." His smile was intimate. "I didn't tell him. Just told him I'd be downstairs in time." He touched his lips to hers. "We're too short on time tonight. Will you see me again?"

"I'd love to." She said it without thinking, then she tried to back up. "That is, I might be busy for a few days, but..."

"Make time." He closed the couple of inches between them and kissed her.

Already she pined for his touch, his kisses. What else could she do?

His tongue entered her mouth and her hand squashed between them, still grasping his cock. She loved the way it hardened between her soft stomach and his taut one. He pushed up against her and she took his cock, lifted up and slid it between her legs. Her pussy, already slick from their previous lovemaking, took him easier this time.

She finished the kiss and sat up. His wicked grin warmed her all the way through and she could have sworn his cock heated up a few degrees. Or perhaps she was the one heating up. His gaze lowered to her breasts and he slowly lifted his hands, as if he couldn't help himself. "Luscious. Gorgeous," he muttered before he cupped them. He simply held her as she began to ride him.

When she leaned back she got the same contact with him as she'd had before. He touched her, his cock rubbing against her sweet spot, the most sensitive part of her body. The spot that sent shivers radiating through her, every part, right down to the tips of her toes. But she kept moving and leaned against his upraised thighs. It gave her the purchase she needed to rise and push, control her drives so even while her body responded to his, she kept the rhythm solid and true. He worked her breasts, pulled and tweaked her nipples and that sent shards of dissonance through the rhythm, the unexpected driving her higher.

They might have entered their own world, so sure was her concentration. She couldn't remember a thing and until he called her name, "Ania!" she hadn't been aware of what it was. It hadn't mattered.

Her body stretched taut, but he never stopped caressing her and he must have felt the moment of stillness before her body combusted. Then he sat up and held her, pushing into her until, with two or three strokes, he came, flooding her with his essence.

They remained still, her legs now curled around him, his legs still supporting her back. Their breath sounded harsh as they regained what they could of their senses. She felt as if she'd run for miles or worked out, which was something she didn't have time for anymore. Soft pleasure added to her euphoria when she realized she couldn't be that much out of shape after all.

And she still wore the garter belt and stockings. She'd bet they were ruined. Out of the corner of her eye she saw a white line tracking up one leg. Oh yeah, but so worth it. She reached up to unhook them.

He moved back to allow her access and when he saw what she was doing, he obliged with the other leg. His touch was far gentler than hers. She reached around to undo the fastening at the back but he arrived before she did and released the hooks with one twist. He touched his lips to hers in a gentle kiss, a startling contrast to a few moments before, and drew away the belt. He glanced down and frowned. "It marked you."

She gave a short laugh. "I guess I've put on a little weight."

He rubbed his palms over the marks and kissed her again. "If you have, it suits you. Don't lose it." He moved and she felt him slip out of her. She failed to stifle her regretful sigh.

"I know, I feel the same way. Come and shower. And don't think this is the end because I have to rush off. I'm not letting you go."

He took her to a luxuriously fitted shower, all white and sparkling silver and glass, with black marble floor and fittings. She'd never seen such a huge room in a hotel, but then, she rarely got to the bedrooms. Unlike some of her employees, she remembered.

"Hey." He must have seen the way her mouth tightened when she thought of her problems. "What's bothering you?"

She avoided his gaze. "Any number of things." She thought of the least of her worries. "Like I failed tonight."

He glanced away to flip on the shower and feel the spray. Satisfied, he drew her inside the large walk-in stall. She gasped at the heat and he adjusted the temperature for her. "Sorry. I like it either very hot or very cold. But I think I can bear it warm. For you. So how do you think you failed tonight?"

He picked up a large sponge and found the complimentary bath gel. A larger bottle than she was used to with the name of a prestigious perfume house on it. Definitely not your regular hotel room.

"I wanted to find something that would tie Sheila to this. I have her on paper, but she was my friend and I still can't believe she's done this to me. I could be in serious trouble. She's done her best to implicate me."

He passed the sponge over her breasts, leaving a trail of scented foam. He was leaning over her, so the water fell either side of them. He proceeded to soap her thoroughly, following the sponge with his hand, washing her as carefully as he caressed her. "You can forget that. I've read you and if you let Chase read you, that'll be enough. You'll have our support."

"I wanted to prove it. I came up here with you because of that. I wanted to see if Sheila was responsible or that bitch Jeanine."

"I'm supposed to meet her for fun and games. She has no fucking idea what fun and games she'll get."

"What will you do?"

He glanced up at her face. "Do you know what Talent Chase Maynord has?"

"Until last year I didn't know he had any, except for making money and running a top-class hotel group. I saw a news report that said he was a Talent but little else."

He paused, the sponge leaking foam down his arm. "Chase is a Sorcerer. He can dissect a mind and take it apart like a surgeon with a scalpel. He works on memory, knowledge and the inner psyche. He'll make sure Jeanine tells us the location of the rogue Bennett lab, one way or another."

"Bennett?"

Johann reached for more shower gel and handed her the reloaded sponge with a smile. "Your turn."

"My pleasure." And it was. It gave her a chance to explore his gorgeous body.

While she worked, he told her about Bennett. "He used to run sleep labs under the protection of the IRDC. You know who they are, right?"

"The International Research and Development Clinics. A charity devoted to discovering the cures to the diseases of the world."

He growled and she glanced up at him in surprise. "A cover for vicious experiments on Talents. They wanted to extract Talents' gifts and sell the result. Magic pills, miracle injections. Now we're forced to work together and we're working to ensure they don't break the law again."

"I never knew." But she wasn't entirely surprised. The IRDC had a fancy office block and hospital downtown and they were secretive about what they did there. Somehow philanthropy toward the third world didn't jive with that image.

"Bennett worked for them until last year. He ran experimental places to investigate and hopefully cure various sleep defects. He came to our notice when he was treating Meghan Armstrong, who is now married to Sandro Gianetti.

He used to be our team leader. Anyway, after the IRDC decided to kidnap Meghan, Sandro stepped in. Bennett turned out to be working his own agenda. The IRDC thought they were providing Talents to him for their experiments, which at the time were hellish enough." He lifted his arm so she could wash under it and around to his shoulders. She had to stretch and he didn't make it easy for her so eventually her breast grazed his chest. He watched her, his gaze burning, while he told her about Bennett. "Now the IRDC has to talk to STORM. They have to develop some kind of working relationship. So they've promised to stop the labs, although for some strange reason we don't quite believe them about that, but we have to pretend we do. Bennett isn't stopping." His mouth curled in a sneer. "In the interests of diplomacy we have to stop him before he makes the IRDC untouchable. They have a lot of money invested in some interesting places and the government, for some reason, doesn't want to close it down. Unlike STORM."

She'd heard the protests that an organization devoted to Talents should be closed down. It wasn't even a government agency, although it seemed to be as inviolate as the FBI or CIA when the spokesmen came forth. It was only that their leader was an ordinary mortal human that STORM was even tolerated in some circles.

He stilled. "I work for STORM."

"You're an agent?"

"Uh-huh. That bother you?"

"I-I don't know. This Talent thing, knowing you've been living among us all this time makes me believe we can carry on doing it. But what you can do—what you are—scares me. And others like me. You could take over the planet."

"You really believe that?" He smiled gently. "I don't have to read your mind to know you don't. We could have taken over, as you put it, at any time. You didn't have to know about us for us to do that. But we didn't because we believe in variety, in co-existence. And there aren't that many of us.

41

Vampires have low fertility and shape-shifters can only have two shape-shifter children. Nature has a way of maintaining a balance."

She said nothing for a moment, but stood under the warm flow as if for a penance, head bowed. "I guess things in LA just got to me. Now Talents have entered the mix and they can be truly obnoxious."

"We're not all the same." He reached for the switch, shutting off the flow. "Come here."

She hadn't realized he'd grabbed a towel until he wrapped it around her. "Why should you think we're the same?" he continued, holding her close, his powerful body keeping her safe. "You have all varieties of human and not every cat is the same, so why should Talents be homogenous?" An edge entered his voice. "That's called bigotry, Ania."

She knew, but she couldn't add anything else. She hadn't met enough Talents to really tell, only watched the documentaries and the news reports. So she stepped out of the shower and walked through to the main room.

He followed, another towel around his waist. He began to rub himself dry so she followed suit. "I'd still like you to stay tonight. Stay here while I go and see Jeanine."

"I can't. I really have to work in the morning." She moved toward him and made a gesture of helplessness. "Look, I'm sorry. I don't really know Talents very well, do I?"

"I can't blame you for that." He dropped the towel and crossed the room to his discarded clothes.

She watched in sheer appreciation of his body before catching herself up. She still didn't know what to do. But she wanted him. "I'll give you my number."

"Never doubt I'll call you. And you know where I'll be."

She knew all right. She'd come back.

Chapter Four

ဆာ

Johann stole several kisses on the way down in the elevator, totally ignoring the guests who got on and off on the way and disregarding Ania's protests. Oblivious to everything but his delightful new lover. This would make the stay in LA far more bearable and perhaps after that. No sense counting his chickens, though. But she'd bowled him over and what he'd seen as a simple distraction had turned into something else. He hadn't even interrogated her properly and kept out of her mind, as he'd promised. Never before had he allowed personal considerations to overwhelm STORM business. He must be slipping.

He'd seen this op as an irritant, but now he was wondering if he couldn't stay over for a while. Or persuade Ania to take a vacation. Oh yeah, that sounded like fun.

By the time they hit the lobby, he had them buttoned-up and virtuous. Within reason. He led the way outside. "I'm meeting La Jeanine in twenty minutes. Plenty of time to see you to your car."

"I didn't come in my car. It's in the garage, getting a new exhaust." Her voice had definitely softened since he'd taken her upstairs. A shame she wouldn't stay.

"A taxi then." He put his hand to the small of her back and guided her toward the side entrance, where the taxis waited.

Before they got there, Johann heard Chase's voice raised in anger. Johann could count the times he'd heard that on the fingers of one hand so he glanced at Ania. She smiled. "Go ahead. I'm sure I can manage to get into a cab without too much trouble."

The voices rose even more. She gave him a little push. "I'm fine. Go."

"Call me. You hear me? Or I'll come looking for you."

"I promise."

Still dissatisfied with the way they had to part, he gave her a brief kiss and turned away.

Johann followed the voice, automatically linking his mind to Chase's as he went.

Jack was there too. He felt his team member's relief and his *Where the fuck have you been?* made him realize he'd not only cut off communication with Ania, he'd shut down all contact since they'd stepped into the shower stall. Although Chase could have broken through if he'd wanted to without much trouble. He reminded Jack of that small fact. *As far as I knew we'd stood down for a couple of hours. Chase could have found me if he needed me. What's up?*

He's going apeshit over this woman. We're supposed to get her to tell us where the lab is, not make it harder to find out. Jeanine wouldn't be ignorant of psi powers. At the very least she'd have a strong mental barrier.

He's lost it.

A smaller side door lay open, leading to a back alley. At least he'd had the sense to take it outside, but this was far from the interrogation they were supposed to undertake. Jesus, what had gotten into Chase? He never blew it like this. Johann closed the door behind him, limiting the damage Chase was doing.

The alley was cast into gloom, illuminated by the lights from the service area of the hotel and the streetlights beyond. The hotel towered behind them and the half moon gleamed above.

He was close enough to hear Chase now. "You want to turn my hotel into a brothel, go ahead. Wait until I get my hands on your boss! I'm going to throw the book at her and sue for damages."

"I told you, I've got a tame reporter. You want this to get to the press, go ahead. My version of it says you knew."

"Can we calm this down?" Jack was doing his best, but his voice had escalated to a gentle roar.

Johann entered the scene to see Chase confronting Jeanine like a fighter waiting for another blow. "Okay, what has she said to you?" He didn't try to raise his voice. Pitching it lower did the trick and Chase stared at him, wild-eyed, before he sighed and raked his fingers through his already disheveled hair.

"A bunch of lies. She wanted me to think my manager was taking a cutback. I know that's not true."

Johann fought for control. Chase had used his psi to ascertain the truth, and in this state, he wasn't sure if Chase was too careful with it. That was why Sorcerers were trained to be cold and unfeeling, but now that Chase had found love, his emotions were emerging after years of frozen inattention. They'd have to be careful with him. Very careful. The problem with freezing your emotions was that you'd never practiced using them. Johann believed in letting rip when he needed to.

"What else?"

"Else? You need *else*?" Chase turned away from him. "You've been working this all around town. You break this, you bring it all down."

"In any case we need something else from you." Johann couldn't get through to Chase. His mind was one red flame and then he saw what had driven Chase wild—oh shit, the woman had gone for the jugular. Jillian.

Jack was careful. *She suggested Jillian was just the type to work with her, actually claimed Jillian had known all about it. You know what Chase is like about her.*

Oh yes. Protective, loving, careful. Johann's eyes narrowed in suspicion. It sounded as if Jeanine was trying to rile Chase. He'd try a distraction. "Why don't you tell me about your little blonde employee?"

He knew his suspicions were right when the woman rounded on him, the light of battle in her eyes. "Did you enjoy her? I'll send my account to you." She cast a triumphant look to Chase. "Your friend finds my services convenient. Why can't you just ignore it?"

But she'd made a tactical mistake and allowed Chase to take two breaths. Time to think. That was all he needed and by the time she turned back to him, his customary glacial expression was beginning to return. But instead of recommencing her attack, she looked over Chase's shoulder, toward the end of the alley, and smiled.

Johann followed her gaze and he froze. Six men headed for them, but that wasn't what chilled him to the bone. The small woman with flyaway blonde hair, glinting where it caught the light from inside the hotel, held between two of the brawny men, did.

Ania kept her head down, but as they passed a bright shaft of light cast by one of the windows, he saw the dark patch on the side of the jaw. Someone would pay for that bruise.

He didn't realize he was growling until Jack cast him a startled glance. He ignored him. "Let her go." He didn't have to raise his voice since they were close enough now.

One man took control of Ania and grinned. "Come here and get her."

Oh sure. But he took a moment to shift. He was vampire all night, but he usually kept his attributes hidden. Now he let his claws out. They sprang out from the sheaths behind his regular fingernails, and he felt the toothbuds just above his eyeteeth itch as his fangs began to emerge. He held them back, ready to use if he needed them. One way or another, tonight he was going to feed. His eyes widened and he knew the red sparks were expanding into flame.

Their opponents stopped but they knew for sure what they'd taken on. Or perhaps not because one turned to another and mouthed, "Vampire?"

He felt the air stir as Jack moved to take center ground. Without looking he knew Chase would take the other side. Although Johann and Jack had all the physical strength, Chase could more than take care of himself in a fight and he'd use his psi. Trouble was, a single blast would wipe everyone out indiscriminately. Too risky in this case and those blasts were hard to control, unlike the cold, considered dissection Chase could also perform. From unconsciousness to death was a small step.

One man held Ania, who struggled in his arms, kicking and writhing. But her soft flat shoes had little impact and the bully who held her merely grinned.

Their gazes caught for a fraught moment and he saw her astonishment. Shit. Then revulsion hit her. Since he'd extended his psi senses he felt it like a slap in the face.

A hard blow to his stomach brought him back to reality and he glanced down, glad his attacker had used the flat of his hand in a karate chop rather than a knife that might stop him while he healed the cut. He bared his teeth and let the tips of his fangs show. The bastard had it coming.

His assailant sucked in a breath but kept coming. Ignoring the sounds of battle coming from all around him, Johann grabbed the man by the neck and lifted. "You know what I am, right?"

The man choked. Rather satisfactorily, Johann thought. "Then why keep coming, you fucking idiot?" He hurled the guy against the nearest wall, careful to avoid the neck. He wanted him alive because he intended to have him for supper. Or part of him.

Jack had his back to him, executing a particularly fine twisting kick that Johann took a moment to admire before he struck out with his left hand, cutting off the man coming in on his left. His hand sank into his attacker's throat, meeting bone and gristle. But this guy was made of tougher stuff than the last one and he kept coming, ducking under the blow and trying to take Johann's legs from under him with one kick to the ankle.

Instead, Johann spread his weight, widening his stance to allow the attacker to think he had a clear strike at his balls. As if. But the man didn't think that far. He kicked up, and at the same time struck out in another karate move, which looked extremely impressive. A shame for him it didn't reach his target, because it would have hurt.

But Johann arrived first. One fast punch to the stomach made his opponent double up. He knew he'd ruptured something, hopefully the liver, with the power of his blow and he felt a couple of ribs crunch in his follow-up punch.

The man dropped to the ground, groaning. Johann glanced around, but the other attackers were down, all but one man who was heading back up the alley as fast as he could, carrying Ania.

He put on a burst of speed and reached the man before he got to the end of the alley.

Steam gushed out of a vent just behind them, separating them from the busy street, and in that moment Johann was on him, pressing close so he could take Ania from him rather than let him drop her. He snaked one arm under her and used the other to pinch the skin on the abductor's neck, exposed by his t-shirt. It crimsoned nicely and he leaned forward and sank his now fully extended fangs into the bastard's carotid.

Not the finest blood he'd ever tasted, but he concentrated on blocking the flow of endorphins into the man's bloodstream, the vampire's usual payment for blood. This fucker didn't deserve it.

Vampires of his age rarely needed more than a few ounces of blood but he took more, weakening the man. He had him in a stranglehold, his thumb over the Adam 's apple and his victim must know what that meant because he didn't resist Johann's assault, even though his hands were free. Which was more than he could say for Ania, who didn't stop struggling.

Stop squirming or he'll drop you!

That sharp command didn't stop her either, so he pressed closer, crushing her between the two male bodies, which constricted her movements enough for him to finish.

When he'd done, Johann moved his thumb over to the other side of the neck and pressed. The prey went limp. He licked the wound enough to stop the man bleeding to death and let him fall to the floor, at the same time taking Ania's weight in his arms.

Jack murmured from behind him, "I thought you were going to kill him."

Chase, in crisper tones, said, "I want three of these in custody. Take them up to floor thirteen."

"Not the penthouse floor then?"

Chase gave Jack a withering stare. "You think?"

Johann took little notice of the exchange, only registered that Chase didn't want his immediate help. In his shape-shifted form, even partially shifted, Jack could handle two of their attackers and Chase could manage one. He had his hands full of Ania's delectable bottom and he didn't want to let go.

But she didn't stop squirming. He gave her a little shake. "Stop it, will you!"

"Put me down, now. Put me down, you—you vampire!"

The vehemence of her words made him stare down at her, startled. Her hair had come out of the hasty knot she'd bundled it into in his room and flowed around her like a halo, catching the light from the street. She looked adorable, despite her expression of furious indignation.

He wanted to lower her gently, so as not to hurt her, but she jerked away and landed on the ground with a soft thud. With an exclamation of distress, he bent to help her up, but she leaped up and jumped away from him, her hands up in a gesture of self-defense. "Keep away from me."

He didn't miss her wince of discomfort when she nearly twisted her ankle in her haste to get away. He would have grabbed her up again if she'd fallen and risked more anger. But why? She knew he was a Talent. Unless her only reason to sleep with him was to soften him up to get something out of him.

Frowning, he stood his ground. "So you whored yourself to me? I should have known better. What the fuck was I thinking?" He lifted his hands and let them slap down again in a gesture of hopelessness.

"Whore?" Her body went still and her gaze lifted to his face. He read fury in them.

Without compunction he entered her mind. Fuck permission, if she'd gotten anything out of him, he needed to know. She could jeopardize the whole operation.

He read nothing but confusion and fury. No cold calculation, no gloating, no sign of victory, which she would have had if she'd succeeded.

Now the woman who'd touched his heart tonight glared at him as if she hated him. He felt it burning at him from her mind and felt relieved that she didn't have any psi powers. Or she would have used them to blast him.

"You don't like vampires?"

She stood up straight and he sensed her putting her mind in order. "You could say that if you were into understatements. Maybe detest and despise is nearer to it."

"Why? You were prepared to sleep with a shape-shifter, so you're not against all Talents. So why vampires?"

The image of a man crossed her mind, fleeting and soon gone. Handsome, young, dark-haired and pale. Was he dead? A past lover killed by a vampire? He couldn't tell because she shut her mind totally and unless he asked Chase to force his way in, Johann had no chance. She firmed her chin. "Because vampires are scum. Okay? If I'd known, if I'd let myself think, I'd never have—" She flushed, her cheeks turning a pretty pink, the cold street lights unable to diminish the soft rose color. Only then did Johann realize someone had joined them.

"We have a problem here." Chase kept his voice low and sent a warning note into Johann's mind. *I don't care what you have going here, get rid of her. Now.*

Johann felt his fangs emerge from their toothbuds. Shit, that was the last thing he needed but sometimes, at times of extreme emotion, they did it on their own. He forced them back, taking a few deep breaths to regain control. "This isn't over, Ania."

"Yes it is." She turned her back and marched off toward the front of the hotel, limping only a little. Johann watched her go and didn't respond to Chase until Ania had climbed into a taxicab. At least he could ensure she was safe although he'd have preferred to see her all the way home. He swept the area telepathically before he turned away. Nothing.

He returned to the end of the alley, back to the dim light where the other two waited for him. They'd moved the bodies there and lined them up. Chase spared them a glance. "They're all alive. I've called for a bus. They can get checked over, then we'll question them before we let the cops have their turn."

"They won't like that."

"Then they should be more alert. They know we're here and they know what I am. And they know about the auction here tonight. Their problem they weren't here, not mine." Chase dismissed the police with a wave of his hand. "Just as well. We need to discuss this."

He gestured to the ground on the other side of the alley to the unconscious men. A body lay in a crumpled heap, the dirt of the alley and blood making a mess of the elegant dress and smooth hairstyle. Jeanine would never sneer at anyone again. And Johann couldn't feel happy about that.

51

Chapter Five

ဢ

Ania looked up at a knock on her office door and quickly hit the shortcut to her screensaver. She didn't want anyone knowing what she'd uncovered. She'd even brought her laptop from home and didn't hook it up to the office system, instead importing the data she needed from a thumb drive. Maybe she was getting paranoid, but not without good reason. Here, in the place she'd thought safe, she'd been used and exploited.

Instead of the office assistant she expected, Andros walked in. As always, she watched his progress across her room, studying his gait. His frown told her he'd noticed. "I'm okay. Well, as okay as ever."

"Did you see the doctor?"

Andros sighed. "I've just come from my hospital checkup." He grimaced. "I've been poked, prodded and stuck with needles, so don't start."

Startled, she swiped her mouse over the mat to activate her laptop to check the date. She groaned. "Oh God, I'm sorry, Andros, I forgot what day it is. I wanted to go with you."

"Thank Christ you did then. You know that I hate fuss. Honestly, it was only a routine checkup. They said I was fine."

Her eyes narrowed. "You'd tell me if you were any worse."

"Sure I would. If you promise not to fuss." He lifted his hand as if to run it through his hair, but dropped it again, no doubt aware that it would ruin his careful style. He'd dyed his blond hair pitch black and parted it on one side, letting the chin-length, rail-straight hair flop over his face. But it had taken straightening treatment and a bucket of hair gel to get it that way. She knew because they shared a bathroom and he went through hair gel as fast as she used sunblock.

She thought he wore more eye makeup than she did, but she had to admit he pulled the look off well. Teamed with black leather and silver, Andros looked good. His thin body and pale face attracted a certain kind of girl and enhanced his position as singer for one of LA's best Emo bands.

He'd dressed carefully today, so she guessed he had a gig later, or maybe he just wanted to put on a good face because although he put on a show of bravado, she knew he hated his hospital checkups.

After leaning over her desk to give her a smacking kiss of greeting, Andros dragged a chair over the floor and sat down by the other side of her desk. "So what's so important you forgot my appointment? You never forget those."

She sighed. "Do you need to ask?"

He grimaced, his mouth turning flat. "No, I guess not. Jeanine's murder."

Just when she'd thought matters couldn't get any worse, they did. Although she hadn't seen Johann since that night two weeks ago, she wasn't surprised he hadn't got in touch. Only a strange regret took her at times, strange because she'd told him to do what he'd actually done. Fucking vampires.

Her secret terror was that someone had seen her that night at the back of the hotel. The further away she could get from that mess the happier she'd be.

A pang went through her as she remembered the Johann from earlier in the evening and the feral monster she'd glimpsed later. He'd terrified her more than the men who'd grabbed her in the process of stepping into a taxi and held her hostage. And that was the real reason she'd asked him not to get in touch with her again. What she'd seen scared the shit out of her and she wasn't used to that, didn't like it at all.

Before that night the only Talents she'd seen that she knew of for sure were the ones on the TV. Even in the club

Andros frequented, The Pit, a place that claimed to be a hangout for vampires, she wasn't sure if any real vampires went there. Of all the Talents outed vampires resisted exposure more than most. Maybe they were just used to hiding. Or they had more to hide than other Talents.

Ania favored the last explanation. If vamps were involved in the scene Andros belonged to, then they had a shitload of stuff to hide. She bit her lip to stop herself saying something she might regret later. But she couldn't resist a "So what are your plans for the rest of the day?"

Andros shrugged and winced a little, pain seizing him momentarily. Ania pretended not to notice, as she had many times before. "I'm rehearsing for a couple of hours later. Meantime, I might go home and get my head down for an hour or two. Exams start soon, my finals, so I need to keep rested." He didn't mention anything else and she didn't nudge him. The missing part of his day lay between them like an open wound, but Ania was too tired to broach it now. Mention it wrong and she'd drive him away for good.

She sighed and turned her attention back to her computer. The figures remained, accusing her of not taking enough notice. Maybe she hadn't. Maybe she deserved all this. But she didn't think so. Nobody did. "I've got some stuff to finish up here. You got your keys?"

Andros grinned and patted his pocket. "One thing I did remember." He was always forgetting his keys to the apartment they shared. "I guess I'll leave you to it then?"

Showing a guileless smiling face got harder every time but Andros didn't seem to notice anything different. They played this game, ignoring each other's deeper hurts because they could hurt each other too much, too hard. They'd ignored it once and she still felt the pain in unguarded moments. For all she knew, he did too.

Andros leaned on the chair arm as he got to his feet. Fatigue was hitting him badly today. Ania's heart went out to him, as it always did, and as he always did, he answered her anxious look with a faint smile. "I'll be okay. I'll just go home and get some rest."

As he headed to the outer door it opened on a knock and admitted the one person Ania prayed she'd never see again, while at the same time praying he wouldn't leave the state. The confusion was driving her mad and now her breath shortened and her temperature went up.

If she wasn't careful he'd notice. She worked to control her admittedly feeble psychic barrier and hoped he wouldn't read her, remembering how he'd promised to help her build a better barrier. She hated this. Hated it.

Johann and Andros stared at each other and then Andros brushed past him and left the room.

Johann remained where he stood, just inside the room. He pushed the door closed behind him without looking at it because all his attention was on her. "What the fuck did you think you were doing?" His first words were spoken in a low, controlled voice, so controlled she knew he was making an effort to keep it that way.

The phone rang, and for once Ania was glad of it. Without giving him the chance to order her to stop, she picked it up. Then wished she hadn't when she heard the voice at the other end of the phone.

"Chase Maynord here. Is this Ania Zelinski?"

"It is." She cleared her throat.

"I believe Johann is on his way to see you, but that is on an entirely different matter. I found a tender for a function at the hotel from your company. Is that right?"

"Yes, it is."

"Normally you'd work with my manager here, but I asked him if I could call you in his stead. I'm calling you now because I want this completely clear. I don't want your company anywhere near any of my hotels."

"But it wasn't—I didn't—"

He went on, breaking into her stuttering denials. "It doesn't matter whether you knew or not. Either way, it looks bad for my hotel that I didn't know or I allowed it. I've made a few enquiries and this has been going on for some time, hasn't it?"

Her gaze strayed to her computer screen. "Yes." She never understood what the phrase "her heart sank" meant until now. Everything inside her felt heavy. "I've been looking at the figures."

"Maybe you should have done that six months ago," he said crisply. "As it is, I had difficulty limiting the damage and I'd advise you to do some too. The word is out that your waitresses provide more than food and drink."

"Yes." Heat flashed through her to think she allowed someone to do this to her. And she knew precisely who. She felt her life crumbling around her.

"And I'm not unaware of what went on between you and Johann. He was there to offer himself up as bait to your pandering manager." Now she wanted to die. The memory of that night had kept her awake at night for the past two weeks, and the way he'd totally failed to get in touch after she'd told him to fuck off. He'd obviously taken her at her word. Until today. "I've kept Johann busy but he wanted to see you when I told him I was calling you. What you do is your concern but believe me when I tell you not to waste your time tendering for business at any of the Timothy hotels."

"I believe you. Will you tell people?"

He paused. "That depends. I want proof that you've put an end to this. I've kept the Timothy group clear of even the suspicion of prostitution." Clearly Chase believed in using unambiguous words. So did she, normally, but she flinched now. "It's clear people know about it already. When I mentioned Simply Service, one of my colleagues resorted to innuendo."

She was finished. She'd had thoughts about calling the bank and getting a loan to tide her over until legitimate service picked up again, but if word had got around she couldn't call it back. She glanced up and then quickly down again, staring at the woodgrain on her desk as if it would tell her something. But she'd find no answers there. Or in her computer. Her only hope was to get out of this with her reputation intact and avoiding bankruptcy.

Staring at her computer screen wouldn't give her any clues, but at least it meant she didn't have to look at Johann. No doubt he'd come to gloat. Or to make sure she did as she was told. Either way, she was about to get another battering. Wasn't she bruised enough already?

Evidently not. But she had to say something in her defense.

"I don't know if you believe me and frankly right now I don't care, but I knew nothing about all this. If that makes me stupid so be it, but I'd rather be stupid than exploitative. I employed young women, college students, as waitresses, not as prostitutes, and I have to find a way to explain to them that their income has stopped. So please, Mr. Maynord, just watch this space and don't pre-empt me. Do that much for me."

She put down the receiver before he had a chance to reply.

Then she braced herself and looked up at Johann. Her gaze met his, dark, intense and so sexy he took her breath away, even now.

"Get out," she said.

He straightened from his leaning posture against the closed door and took a step forward. She remained where she was, didn't give him the satisfaction of showing her leap of fear. She knew what he was now and she'd never, knowingly, been so close to a vampire before, never been so aware of the red-hot passion lurking beneath the surface. But however hard she tried she couldn't forget his tenderness as well as his passion.

"I tried to keep away. One fun session with you—what were the odds it would turn into something else? But it has, Ania, and you know it as well as I do. We need to clear the air, at the very least."

His voice sent a shiver of recognition through her body. Almost despite herself it yearned for him. Skin to skin. How could she remember that at a time like this?

"I've investigated you, mostly the traditional way. After you showed up that night Chase tried to persuade me you were a plant. It worked out, didn't it? You seduced me, kept me away from the action then turned up as a hostage to distract me. The way you treated me afterward added to that. But Chase didn't bother reading you below the superficial. I did."

She shivered again, suddenly cold. He knew too much, saw too much.

He gazed at her under half-closed lids, his eyes glittering. Anger or speculation? She couldn't tell. "When I took you to my suite, I read no subterfuge and I would have done so. I'm a trained agent—I'm used to looking for these things in other peoples' minds. You were either very good or honest. When we made love, it blew me apart, but that was because you gave yourself to me honestly. I have no doubt about that. But that didn't mean you weren't just enjoying your job, did it? You had a year off work, so what you told me could have been true. Or you could have been directing the whole thing from behind the scenes." He spread his hands and she remembered how they'd felt spread over her buttocks, urging her to take him deeper. She blocked the thought. She couldn't afford weakness now. "But I read you and either I'm right or I'm not Johann Kovacs. Everything I have, everything I felt told me you were on the level. I had to make a choice, so I did. And I came here."

Relief flooded her so fully she nearly sagged forward as her muscles lost their tension. He believed her, still believed her. His absence in the past two weeks convinced her that she'd lost her only ally. She'd stormed out of his life because the sight of him in full vampire mode, tearing the throat out of one of her assailants, had terrified her. She wanted no part of it, so she'd left, needing to think. She still hadn't reached any conclusions.

"I want to ask you a few things."

She shrugged. "Ask away." She couldn't throw him out, she couldn't stop him asking his questions but she wouldn't answer if she didn't want to.

"The man who just left. He's sick."

That wasn't a question. "Yes."

"Then I'm sorry. It's a serious illness. I didn't have to enter his mind to know — I could smell it."

Her eyes widened. "Are you saying he stinks?"

A slight smile tugged at his lips, soon gone. "Only to someone like me. When there's a problem with the blood, it alerts us."

"You can't drink tainted blood." She allowed her mouth to tighten in a sneer.

"Best not to." The smile returned. "But we don't drink blood. Ever seen what blood can do to the digestive system?"

"On the whole, I prefer not to think about it."

"It could make you very ill. We ingest it, draw it up the hollow centers of the fangs. Just the small amount we need. Did you know Congress is discussing licensing vampires? They're afraid we'll pass on disease. Now we have to show them that we can't. They might still want us licensed." He sighed. "And we're wasting our time on shits like Bennett." He paused and stared at her, another realization coming to his mind. "And that man is your brother."

Johann knew he'd hit paydirt when he saw Ania flinch and then recover. He hadn't needed to enter the man's mind to recognize the relationship between the two. Despite the dyed black hair and the slouching posture they shared too many of the same characteristics—the blue eyes, the pale skin, the shape of the face with the pointed chin and wide cheekbones. In his investigations he'd seen pictures of Andros as a blond-haired gangly teenager. Now in his early twenties, he'd done his best to alter his appearance but he was still unmistakably Ania's brother. "Did you think I wouldn't notice?"

She looked away and it was like removing the light from the room. "Did you read his mind?"

He let his mouth relax in another smile. He couldn't help it, just being in her presence warmed him. "A little. Only superficially."

She frowned. "I thought vampires only had their powers at night?"

That made him laugh outright. "You make me sound like a comic book hero! Powers, huh? If you mean I grow fangs and increase my strength after sunset, then yeah. But telepathy and a few other things remain all day. Oh yes, and I can't flash in the daytime."

This time she very nearly smiled. His desire to see those lips curve increased. "You flash?"

"I don't expose myself in public, no. I do move from place to place in an instant. Within reason. But not in daytime." He glanced out the window. "Certainly not in the blazing LA sunshine."

"How does—never mind." She put up her chin. He wanted to taste it, flick his tongue over it on his way to her mouth. "I won't talk to you. You're a vampire. I despise vampires."

"No you don't."

"Where have you been?" Her cheeks flushed red, then paled again. He took another step forward, he was nearly touching her desk now. "It's been a fortnight since we—"

"Made love? Fucked? How are you justifying it in your mind?" He really wanted to know that. Because he didn't think of it as just fucking. They'd connected at a deeper level, or he'd thought so, anyhow.

At least he'd brought that pretty flush back to her cheeks. He studied her face. Her makeup, hastily applied, hadn't concealed the dark shadows under her eyes or the pallor of her features, more than the natural paleness of her skin. He didn't like that look and he didn't like that it concerned him. "You're tired."

Her brows snapped together. "Is it any wonder? With Andros ill and my business falling apart around me?"

Johann sat on the chair in front of the desk and crossed his legs, his left ankle resting on his right thigh. He stared at the tip of his black boot, mildly annoyed that he'd manage to scuff the toe on a brand new pair. "Tell me then. See if I can help you."

That made her frown more. "How can you help me? You're a vampire."

"And you're sounding more and more like a bigoted zealot." But he'd met the real thing, the person who couldn't see beyond what he was to who he was. Even before they'd been outed last year, some people had known and they didn't all like what they heard. Some were still in denial, refusing to accept any of it. They'd spent so long persuading the public that stories about vampires and dragons were just that— stories—that some people found it hard to believe. He couldn't blame them. He'd been one of the naysayers—if he'd had his way they'd still be underground. But in the end, the outing hadn't come from the inside. A TV documentary, a collection of sightings and the deed was done. All Talents had to do was refuse to deny it.

Easy as that. A thousand years and more of hiding gone, overnight.

Now Ania looked away, back to that computer screen. He couldn't see it from where he was sitting, and if he stood up to look, she'd close it down. What did it hold? A letter, accounts? He'd guess the latter because that little furrow between her brows deepened every time she looked at it. He ached to kiss it away.

She glanced back at him. "I'm not a bigot. Or a zealot. I've never been drawn to extremes in religion or politics."

"Then stop thinking of Talents as a homogenous whole. We're people, just like you, and we're different, just like you. There are a few cultural quirks, natural developments from either our nature or the way we were brought up to hide part of what we are, but we're here and we're real."

He didn't move. Just met her gaze and kept it. Let her see. Eventually she gave a little sigh that made her breasts lift a little in the confines of the soft white blouse she wore. She probably thought it was a businesslike garment, but he could see the lines of her lace bra and even the shadow of her delicious nipples. Maybe he was imagining those. The sight was seared on his memory for all time.

He flicked his gaze back to her face but didn't hide where he'd been looking. He wanted to touch her cheek, see if that pink meant she'd heated.

"Ania, we're not all the same."

"All the vampires I've known have been the same."

Johann went on alert. Generalizations abandoned, she was talking about a particular group and he had a strong idea where they hung out. "Who, Ania?" He used her name again, reminding her of the way he'd spoken it when they'd shared a bed — with tenderness and care.

"People Andros knows."

"Tell me about them."

She closed her eyes and touched her fingers to the bridge of her nose in a gesture of utter surrender. That was too much. In an instant Johann had risen to his feet and strode to her side of the desk. Her desk chair was armless and sturdy, so he swept her up and sat down with her on his lap. He wouldn't watch her suffer anymore.

Stiffening, she sat up but he urged her back, curving his arms around her waist. "No, don't push me away. I hate to see you this tired, as if the weight of the world rests on your shoulders. Lean on me, at least for now." He brushed a kiss over her forehead, a mere touch of his lips to her skin. Even that made his cock stir. "Tell me about your brother and his friends."

She snuggled against him before she pulled away again, but he made it clear he wasn't about to let her go so she sighed again and relaxed. Only this sigh sounded as if it had a little more contentment in it.

"It's my brother. He's so ill." He sensed her love for her family, knew from personal experience that expats tended to stick together, to put a lot of emphasis on family.

"What's wrong with him?"

"He has muscular dystrophy. Becker's Syndrome to be precise." Johann sucked in a breath and she lifted her chin to look up at his face. "You know what that means?"

"Some."

"So you know this will kill him eventually. Becker's affects young men. They get it through their mothers. It becomes apparent in their twenties."

"Does anybody else in your family have it?"

She shrugged, the movement a caress against his chest. "Hard to say. We lost a lot of the family. My mother's family were Jewish and most of them died in the concentration camps in World War Two. The survivors came to the States after the war. My grandparents."

He remembered that time. He'd even spent a little time in a camp, arrested as a mental defective because of his telepathic ability. They'd wanted to experiment on him. He'd fed from the guards and escaped within a couple of months of incarceration, flashed out. Shame still swept him when he remembered how many he'd left behind, that he couldn't take them with him. He'd been too ill himself to do much to help. Flashing took a lot of energy. So he just grunted, to tell her he understood, and stroked her arm to show her he cared.

"They carried the gene and now Andros has it. He'll die, Johann, and he's the only family I have left. Now." She took a deep breath and he knew she was sucking back the tears.

"Do you want me to read you on this? Just take it from your mind?"

"No!" She sounded scared.

He wouldn't do it, just for that reason. "Tell me then. I promise I won't enter your mind without permission."

"You swear it?"

"I do." It would hurt, but he'd keep completely out of her mind if it meant gaining her trust, something he needed badly.

She took a great shuddering sigh before she went on. The tension in her body told him how hard she was fighting tears. "Okay. Andros is four years younger than me and he's a member of a band as well as studying at college. He's doing well with both, or he was before the MD kicked in. It makes him tired. And it also depresses him." She swallowed. Johann so wanted to enter her mind, because at least he could soothe her a little. But he'd promised. She went on. "He doesn't know how much longer he has, you see. It started in his teens, but Becker's doesn't work as fast as Duchene's and it went a couple of years before it was diagnosed. He just thought he was getting more tired than usual and the aches were just growing pains. But once he got into his twenties we couldn't ignore it anymore."

"So he took longer at university and you've supported him all this time."

She nodded, the movement caressing him. He felt the movement and although he knew she didn't mean to arouse, he felt tenderness rising in him. He wanted to love her slowly, make her feel better. But although he held her now he doubted she'd let him.

"Two years ago my mother got cancer. Leukemia." Johann held her tighter as if somehow that would help to ease her pain. "She died three months ago, but while she was ill she needed me. My dad died when I was twelve, so she didn't have anyone else. Andros could hardly do it. During her last year she needed a caregiver, and I was it. I was only glad that Sheila, my business partner, could take over during Mom's illness." She stirred and he loosened his hold a little, afraid he might be hurting her, unable to tell. "Simply Service did well, made profits and I thought I could afford to take the time to care for my mom. The business did even better and Sheila took care of the expansion we'd planned. Profits were good. I didn't know why until a month ago." She closed her eyes. "I can't believe I was such an idiot."

"That is ridiculous." That completed the picture. She took extended leave to care for her mother and Sheila Murtagh had taken advantage. "Did you know Sheila before you went into business with her?"

"Yes. We were schoolfriends. She did well at school, great at math and we started the business with a fifty-fifty finance split. She inherited some money and my mother backed me. We'd been going for four years when my mom got ill. Sheila just kept me updated." She gestured at the computer screen, now showing a selection of family photos on the screensaver. "I didn't realize she was so selective with her updating." Extending a finger, she shifted the mouse and activated the screen. "You can look if you like."

"Is there any need?"

"Just proof."

65

"I don't need proof. Tell me what she did."

Ania stared at him, her face a picture of astonishment, blue eyes wide, mouth parted. So he kissed her. How could he resist? So open, soft and beautiful, and needy, although she tried hard to hide it.

He drew back after a gentle taste and smiled at her, satisfied that desperate edge had gone from her eyes. "She kept the prostitution separate from the waitress service?"

She licked her lips and he groaned. "Don't do that. I'm supposed to be interrogating you."

She brought her wrists to the front of her body, held them together and sat up straight. The movement brought her sweet ass rubbing against his cock, and although he'd been working hard at not getting aroused, he could pretty much call that attempt a failure now. He hardened, rigid now. "You should handcuff me."

"I should." He gave her a wolfish smile. "Do you want me to?"

He watched her swallow and imagined her swallowing something else. "I've never thought of it before, but I don't know, I never—"

"Hey." He lifted his hand to grasp her wrists. They were so small and slim, that pale skin so easy to bruise. It scared him to death, the thought that he might really hurt her, but at the same time, the idea of having her in his control, under his power, turned him on even more than he was already. He kissed her jaw where the bastards had bruised her that night in the alley. It was as porcelain pale as the rest of her skin now.

She did him in. He had to concentrate, not think about having her, taking her. Worse than a two-hundred-pound gorilla in the middle of the room. But he'd try.

"Can we finish this?"

The innocent look she cast him was wholly false. "Finish what exactly?"

He saw the lift in her mood from utter dejection to faint hope and realized perhaps that was the way to help her. Show her she was desired, wanted, appreciated.

"Tell me how the business got out of hand. Do it now. Please."

When the stricken look returned he felt like shit, but he had to do it. Lives were at stake. She glanced at the computer screen. "Toward the end, Mom didn't sleep well and I was running on empty. I think Sheila escalated the business then and siphoned the money into our joint savings account, then took it from there."

"Nursing someone through a chronic illness means you're short of sleep all the time. You were under stress as well. It's no wonder you saw the success of Simply Service as just one less thing to worry about."

She rested her forehead on his shoulder. "But I should have noticed something. At the time I was relieved I didn't have money worries on top of everything else." She grimaced. "Not like I have now."

"How much do you have left?"

"Not enough. I've been juggling money for the last couple of weeks, but the work's dried up and I can't do it anymore."

The trembling of her jaw alerted him before she clenched it tight and blinked hard. He wouldn't let on that he'd seen her weakness. "That night at the Timothy hotel, I went to the function. I couldn't believe what I suspected, so I decided to go — undercover, I suppose, and find out for myself. Jeanine was one of the new managers and none of her team knew me so I signed on for the night. The only person who knew me there was Chase Maynord and I managed to avoid him until later. What I found out showed me how it was worked. I knew I was ruined."

"So where's Sheila now?"

Ania shrugged. "Gone. Left her apartment, emptied her accounts. A planned bolt."

Chapter Six

౬౧

He'd suspected as much. Sheila Murtagh had gone and left Ania to take the brunt of the mess. What she didn't know was the link between Simply Service and The Pit. He'd have to tell her.

"Ania, there's more." She stiffened again. "Remember that we're here to track down Bennett and his labs?" She nodded, her hair clinging to the fabric of his t-shirt. His fingers itched to stroke that silky mass but he held off. "Sheila Murtagh had a financial connection with The Pit."

She tipped her head and her eyes widened in surprise. "The place Andros goes to? The vampire club?"

He nodded grimly. "That's the one. We knew about Andros' connection and your connection so we were concentrating on you. Until we discovered Sheila's financial connection it seemed likely you were the link we needed. Several vampires have disappeared from the area recently, a sure sign there's a lab in the vicinity, and since the IRDC assure us they've closed all their labs down, pending legal suits to reopen them, it could only be Bennett. Or the IRDC people were lying of course. It wouldn't be the first time. Either way, we had an active lab and we want to shut it down."

"'We' being STORM?"

"Yep." Their gazes met, clashed. "We need Bennett. His roots are far deeper than we thought." They'd find him. Anything else was unthinkable. Bennett had made a big mistake when he'd killed two IRDC agents. Now they were after him too.

Which reminded him of something he had to ask her, although the feel of her warm, soft body against his was driving him to distraction.

Fuck it, it could wait. He drew her down and gave her a soft kiss, pleased when she didn't recoil. She was getting over her aversion to him. As long as he kept his human form. If he went vampire, which was impossible at the moment anyway, he wasn't sure if she'd stay with him.

He closed the inch or two that lay between their mouths to kiss her again. This time he tightened his hold around her waist and kept her close, enjoying the sensation of her soft lips against his, before he opened her mouth with a flick of his tongue. Then plunged within to taste a little paradise.

When they parted, he kept her close and she stared at him, her gaze roaming over his face. "You don't look like a vampire now."

"I'm sorry I shocked you so badly. It was the last thing I wanted to do but I had no choice. I thought you'd gone."

"They grabbed me just before I stepped into the taxi. I was glad to see you until — until — "

"Until I turned vampire." He curved his free hand around her breast at the side, relief flooding him when she didn't move away. He loved the way she felt. He'd never felt such an odd mixture of calm and excitement before and he found he liked it. She took her lower lip between her teeth and released the plump morsel again. He leaned forward to touch his tongue to the place. "But it's daytime now. So I'm just a man."

Her lashes lowered again and faint color tinged her cheeks. "I wouldn't say 'just'."

He chuckled. "Thank you for that," and unable to resist, took her mouth again. This time he cupped her breast and felt the wonder of her giving flesh under his hand. She felt so small, so delicate, and he loved the sensation of cherishing her, not a feeling Johann was used to where sex was concerned.

Most of his sexual activities were more like a duel, especially with females of his species, who loved to fight back.

But Ania wasn't exactly a passive partner. Her hands curved around his face, keeping him in place while they kissed. He caressed her, taking particular care to notice when she flinched or when she flowed under his hands. Discovering a woman without resorting to even a superficial mental reading was something else. Something new. His telepathy was another of his senses, one he often took for granted, but without it he had to fall back on the others.

The experience intrigued him. Not only that, it made him hungry. For more of her, to explore her, touch her, smell her, taste her. But did she want this?

With an effort and a lingering caress of his lips, he drew back enough to study her face. "I want you, Ania. But I won't do this if you're scared or doubtful. I'd rather wait until you're ready."

Her gaze seemed ready to him, her eyes wide and dewy, her lips slightly open and flushed with his kisses. That pretty blush lingered on her cheekbones and her earlobes, he noticed, were pink. He wanted to take them into his mouth and bite down. Would she allow it? Her breath came shallowly, sending gusts of air across his face. He wanted to feel that on other parts of his body.

He waited, forcing himself not to move until she gave her answer. He couldn't push her now, otherwise she'd never trust him, but he so wanted this. Nothing existed for him now except the reality of making love to Ania.

"Why would you do that? Wait, I mean?"

He frowned. "Because I think you have enough problems without me forcing myself on you."

"What do you want?"

"I want to know that you want me. That's all."

She lifted her finger, slightly trembling, and touched it to his lips. "Can't you tell?"

"It's not enough. I won't enter your mind without your permission since you dislike it so much. I won't do anything you don't want." He sucked her finger into his mouth, licked the tip and felt her shudder. His hands went to her blouse and slowly, with great concentration, he undid the first button.

She lowered her chin and watched, then raised her gaze to his face. "That's what I want. Make me feel better. I've felt so bad for so long, I deserve this. To feel good for a little while, even if it's only half an hour."

"Did you feel good when we made love before?"

She smiled, then it was gone. "Yes. Better than I've felt for years."

Years?

So he undid the rest of the buttons, taking his time over them all. If he had his way, this would last longer than a half-hour. He'd make her feel good, then he'd make sure she slept, and hold her. Exhaustion lined her eyes, put lines that shouldn't rightly be there on her face. He wanted them gone.

She wore a pretty lace bra that he took a moment to admire. The way her nipples peaked against the white lace and the underwires pushed her breasts up into an enticing cleavage. He enjoyed the sight and kissed between her breasts, licked into the cleavage, savoring the taste of her. But the desire to have her bare overrode his enjoyment of aesthetics so he reached around her to find the back fastening. He was good at those. He had it unclipped in a second.

Urging her to sit up, he divested her of the blouse and bra. She sat on his lap, deliciously naked from the waist up, the window behind her and the door unlocked. Would she object?

She licked her lips and glanced over his shoulder at the rows of windows in the building across the street. "They could see me."

"If they're looking. You want the blinds closed?" He watched her carefully, gauging her response.

She glanced over his head again. "I think so." Leaning over him, she grabbed the control and the blinds dropped over the windows behind her. Pity, because Johann enjoyed the tingle of awareness. He doubted anyone could see much anyway, because she didn't have any lights on in the office and the chair sat at least two feet away from the windows. But he took advantage of her position to place a string of kisses around her nipple before he took the tip into his mouth for a kiss of greeting. He was glad of the opportunity to re-acquaint himself with it and the rest of her.

But he didn't want to do it in the dark or the near dark so he looked for the control on the large desk-lamp that craned over the table and turned it on.

She looked gorgeous in the spotlight. Laughing, she altered the shade until the light shone onto the table. He growled and attacked, but took care to do it in a soft, non-threatening way, keeping the laughter in his tone. Right now she didn't need full-on passion, she didn't need roughness, she needed healing. And he was the one to heal her.

He urged her down to his mouth again and kissed her while she explored his chest and pushed his shirt off his shoulders. He got to his feet, taking her with him, and pressed their bodies together. Those pretty nipples, hard against his chest, would drive him crazy. She wriggled and they moved, abrading his skin until he groaned into their kiss.

The zipper to her skirt was in back, so he slid it down and undid the button at the top. The skirt slid away.

Blessed be, she was wearing stockings and a garter belt again. He felt them under his hands, toyed with the satin-covered elastic and let his fingers play. Soft skin gave way to lacy tops, then the stockings with their slightly rough edge. The textures enticed him while he kissed her, his tongue playing in her mouth, tracing her lips to return to the sweet depths. He felt her hands at his waistband and felt her release him, then lower his shorts with fumbling hands and take hold of him. He flinched and drew back to take a breath, but he couldn't prevent his lips curving into a smile. "Now that's what I'm talking about," he said, softer than a sigh, and saw her responding smile with pleasure blooming in his heart. Sheer pleasure, and at that moment he thought that was all he needed.

But he knew he was lying to himself when her fingers closed around his cock. *That* was what he wanted. He kissed her, kept it soft and knew his lips were trembling with need. He couldn't wait much longer now, not when she did that thing with her fingertips, stroking his liquid over his cock, making the slippery head ready to take her.

He touched her, slid his finger between the lips of her pussy. "*Miláčku*, you're soaking."

"You're surprised? When you do this to me?" She touched her lips to his cheek, so softly he wanted to close his eyes and save the moment forever. One of those perfect moments out of time that came so rarely, even in a life as long as his.

He smiled and moved his fingers a little, feeling her melt around him. Now. He needed her now.

After glancing behind her, he urged her back and then leaned her against his arm so she lowered slowly to her desk. The only thing under her was wood. Her laptop was on one side of her and the lamp on the other, illuminating her fabulous curvy body.

Her legs opened, enclosing his, and he guided his cock with one hand until it met her body, slid down and inside her. He had to push to get the flared head past her opening, then it was all sugar.

Hot, liquid honey, to be precise. He pushed farther into her and didn't stop until he was all the way in. "You are something, lady."

She laughed at his words and then half closed her eyes and sighed. "That's the best I've felt all day."

"Oh yeah, me too." This almost made up for the shitty couple of weeks he'd had thinking about her and keeping away from her. No more. He was moving in close and personal and it didn't get much more personal than this.

He leaned over her, planting his hands on either side of her head before bending for another of her addictive kisses. Her warm, soft body quivered against his, and as he set up the driving rhythm designed to take them higher, her stomach muscles tightened. Hell, she was nearly there already.

So was he. But he didn't intend to go off like some fifteen-year-old with his first girl. He'd make this last. He wanted two orgasms out of her at least before he'd let himself go.

The first one came fast and hard and the way her pussy clenched around his cock nearly finished him. Fast compressions clamped tight and he threw back his head to try to control his breathing while Ania went wild under him. The way she held him tight, as if she'd never let him go, warmed him while his body heated and howled, begging for release.

Not yet. Shit, not yet.

She finished with tiny quivers and flutters and smiled up at him, her blue eyes glowing. "Wow."

"We've not finished yet," he said when he'd unclamped his jaw. Thankfully, he was still hard inside her though it had been a close-run thing.

He wanted more and he wanted her soft and sweet and melting. He wanted to love her to sleep.

But first he wanted to love her to a screaming frenzy.

Alarm shaded her eyes. "The door, it's not locked."

"Nobody will come in." He tried to keep his voice low and soothing. Actually, it being daytime, the only psi sense he had was telepathy, so he wasn't sure at all. But chances were that no one would disturb them. He'd have to rely on that.

"Promise?"

Slowly, he shook his head. "But I'll promise you this. You're coming again."

She laughed and lifted her legs. One of them had her skirt tangled around it but it didn't stop her curving them over his ass and tightening them so he drove deep, deep inside her. "Make me."

This laughing, lush nymph was the opposite of the angst-ridden female he'd confronted a short while earlier. While sex didn't cure anything, it didn't hurt either.

He lifted the top part of his body so he could watch her breasts quiver as he thrust inside her and then balanced on one hand so he could touch her.

So good, so smooth. He watched his hand slip down her body, between her breasts, pausing to circle her sweet navel and down farther still to tangle with the short hair barely covering her pussy. Clipped and bikini'd into submission, he guessed. And loved it. Perhaps she'd let him shave her. At the thought something inside him snapped. Too good to pass up, he'd watch her from closer quarters.

Very much closer. He pulled out and thrust, hearing the wet contact their bodies made, smelling their joint arousal, and he knew this time he wouldn't be able to do anything but lose control.

So he fucked her stupid. Or himself. This way of doing it, without mental contact, roused the animal in him and he went with it, loving it. His other senses went into overdrive. The sight of her, spotlighted by the desk lamp, and the small sounds she was making drove him to push harder, until his balls made firm contact with her backside with every stroke. The extra stimulation, that slap at the end of every stroke finally broke him. He felt the tension build inside him and glanced down at Ania to see her taking him, pulling him in with her legs locked around him. She reached a hand up to him as if she were drowning and he took it as if he were joining her.

In another few seconds, he did. When he felt her clench around him again in a spasm of ecstasy, his cock stiffened, then detonated in a paroxysm of joy.

Johann collapsed over her, only remembering at the last moment to take his weight on his elbows. It was all he could do. One hand clasping hers, their fingers intertwined, they lay on her desk. The clasp of her legs loosened.

He felt her damp kiss on his neck, which he assumed was probably damp too. She kissed him again, paused, then shifted. Shit, he must be heavy on her. He stood, using one hand to support himself, and felt her chair at the back of his knees, so he sat, tugging her to join him. With a smile, she managed it, curling up on his lap.

Wonderful, he felt wonderful. Folding her into his arms, he felt her heart beating against his, the rapid rhythm a counterpart to their slowly steadying breaths.

He laughed, low and shaky. "Shit, I need a shower."

She laughed too. "This isn't what you might call a luxury office, Johann. We put all the money into the business."

Her body tensed and he knew she'd remembered all he'd tried to help her forget. But she wouldn't forget it completely until she could put it behind her, he knew that too. Perhaps she'd want to put him behind her with it. Perhaps he'd want to do the same. But for now, he couldn't imagine anywhere else he'd rather be, anyone he'd rather be with. So he held her and memorized the way her body curled into his, the way she let him support them both. "You are beautiful," he told her.

Her chuckle showed him what she thought of that. "Then you're blind."

"Perhaps you are, that you don't see it."

He held her a while longer and they exchanged soft kisses and sweet talk. Johann couldn't remember the last time he'd taken time with a lover like this. Usually he couldn't wait to leave after fucking, but this time he had the strangest desire to hold her and cuddle her, keep her close and safe.

But they couldn't stay here. "Come back to the hotel with me. We'll shower and eat."

She snuggled against him and he felt his cock stir. "My apartment's closer and Andros won't be back for a while. He's gone to college, then he has a gig tonight. Come home with me."

He stroked her hair back from her face. "Are you sure?"

"Yes."

They helped each other to dress and his hands lingered over her when he wanted to strip her again. He couldn't believe how he was feeling, but maybe it was because she wouldn't let him read her. She'd kept the mystique that way. He wanted more.

Her car turned out to be an old Chevy, but it worked well enough and she cranked up the aircon to cope with the heat of the day outside. She brought her laptop with her and locked the office up when they left.

She and Andros lived in the Palms, the oldest part of LA, and one that had seen better, more glamorous days. Johann felt a pang of sadness when he saw the rows of McMansions and apartment blocks and recalled the old days. He'd seen this area in the fifties, when it still held remnants of the glory of the thirties and not all the glamorous residents had moved out to Beverly Hills. Remnants of the old place remained in the occasional Mexican-style old building and a touch of quaint architecture here and there. Still, people had to live somewhere and he was relieved to find that Ania and her brother weren't so poor that they had to leave to somewhere sleazy. With this amendment to their fortunes, that could change.

But not if he could help it.

She parked in a small lot at the rear of the building and he stepped out of the car into the blinding sunshine, remembering to put on his heavy-duty shades before he exited the car.

Ania grinned at him before she tilted her own graduated sunglasses over her nose. "Weird. I always thought you people couldn't go out in the sun." He appreciated that she didn't say the dreaded V word where someone might hear her. He still wasn't comfortable with being stared at once people knew what he was. They didn't care *who* he was once they found out the *what* part of it.

He rounded the trunk of the car and joined her. "You're half right. My other half has never seen the sun. Never likely to either. Some of us live wholly in the dark, but I like to see the sun."

"So what do you do for vitamin D?"

"Vitamins. I'm not the night owl type. Not completely, anyway, so I'll do my share of sun worshiping."

The building turned out nondescript, but clean. No super on the door, he noted. In the current circumstances he didn't like that. They took the elevator to the second floor and she took her key out of a pocket at the front of her laptop case. "Welcome to my small patch of LA."

He was smiling when she opened the door, then he grabbed her and shoved her out of the way. "Stay back."

"What's wrong?"

"You've had a break-in."

Chapter Seven

&

Ania craned her neck to see past Johann, unable to break out of the hold he had on her. He held her arm in one hand, not enough to bruise, but hard enough to restrain her. Or protect her, she wasn't sure which.

"It all looks normal to me, just like I left it this morning."

He turned around then and stared at her. "Are you serious?"

She glanced at the room beyond him. "I know it's a bit untidy, but it's not that bad." She took advantage of his temporary stunned state to pull herself free and walk past him into the room.

Maybe it was a bit more untidy than usual, but her coffee cup was still on the table, and the wineglass from last night. Andros must have cleared away the pizza dish they'd shared from while they watched TV. She doubted any burglar would take that and not one of the boxes that were stacked up in the corners of the room, next to the teetering piles of books where she'd half unpacked before realizing what a hopeless task it was. At least she knew where her unread novels were now. That had bothered her.

Johann stood in the middle of the room and turned around. "This is a student apartment," he said. He sounded dazed.

"It's a large one. Two bedrooms."

"And you're trying to cram the contents of a large house into it." He eyed the huge wooden bookcase doubtfully, as if it would fall on him any moment. There was no chance of that. Well, not much of a chance, anyway. She'd made sure to put the biggest books at the bottom.

"I sold the family home to help with the business and to pay for Mom's treatment but I couldn't bear to part with everything. Some of it is in storage," she said helpfully. "I just kept a few things here that I couldn't do without."

He blinked and then looked at her and grinned. "I guess students are just untidy by nature."

"Um." She couldn't let him disparage Andros like that so she took his hand and led him across the room to the door leading to the tiny hallway that held the bedroom and bathroom doors. She opened a door. "This is Andros' room."

Johann stared at the pin-neat bedroom. "Ah."

"I'm afraid it's me. Andros hates my mess but he puts up with it because he knows I need to be near him. I guess I didn't realize how much I'd gotten used to living in big spaces."

"Why don't you pay someone to come in and clean up for you?"

She gently closed Andros' door. "We did. She took one look and said she wouldn't do it for double the usual rate."

"I can understand that."

"You don't have stuff?"

Slowly, he shook his head. "Not like this. I guess we Talents got used to leaving things behind and starting again. I have friends who manage to keep hold of things, but not like this. They keep mementoes, or maybe jewelry and antique furniture. Not—"

He stopped suddenly and she knew what he was about to say. Garbage. Perhaps to him it was, but to her it meant more than that. It meant her happy childhood, loving parents, when everything seemed sunnier. Not like now. Especially not like now.

Sighing, she knew he had to see the worst. So she opened the door opposite to Andros' and let Johann look at the full horror inside.

Silence fell for a full minute. The bed covered in clothes she'd discarded, the drawers crammed to overflowing, the inevitable piles of books and magazines. And the jumble of toiletries and jewelry on the vanity. She'd left her closet open, so he could see the glory there too. His Adam's apple bobbed when he swallowed. "Okay, that's it. Pack a bag."

"What?"

He bit his lip and turned to face her. "I didn't mean it to come out like that, but I have no intention of leaving you alone until this business is over and we've caught the people who want to hurt you."

She frowned, disliking his peremptory command. "Who wants to hurt me?"

"They know you. They held you hostage to try to stop me fighting them. They know we're—well, they know." When she heard the slight hesitation, her heart sank. "You're not safe yet."

"You've been watching us? Spying on us?"

That shadowing in his eyes told her she was right. "You're too smart, you know that? Yes, okay, that as well. We kept an eye on you for your own safety, or rather the others did. After you told me to get lost, I figured you wouldn't like the idea of me being on the detail." There was something else. She saw the shade of that pass over his face and she didn't have to be a mind reader to know what he meant. She'd seen that look before. The "This is fun, don't let's get too involved" look.

Since he was in a truth-telling mood, she wanted to know more. "So what exactly do you know about me and Andros?"

"Your brother, very little. We knew who he was, and that he's a student at UCLA, that's all. And no criminal record. I stayed away from you until I couldn't stand it anymore. I couldn't get you out of my mind, so I came back." He gave her a smoldering look that threatened to singe her clothes off where she stood. "And I was right. There's something between us."

"Sex?" she suggested sweetly.

"Something more than that. Sex I can take or leave. But not with you."

Well that put her in her place. A vampire's toy. And to her absolute disgust, she thrilled to the idea. The feminist in her rebelled at the thought, but her secret self, the one she'd never let loose, wanted it badly. Her panties dampened and she wrenched her thoughts away.

Not soon enough. Although he wasn't in her mind, he didn't need to be. He pulled her close and gave her a brief, hard kiss. "That's on account. We are definitely going to play."

She put a hand on his chest and felt the warmth under his shirt. "Do you hypnotize people? There's a vampire blog that says you do."

He gave her a slow smile. "What do you think? Is it easier to blame others for your mistakes, say you were hypnotized into it? You know we have telepathy and some of us can, if we want to, persuade. But not force you to do anything you don't want to do. That's called compulsion and it's illegal." He grimaced. "It used to be punishable by death, but now, who knows?"

"So no hypnotism."

"Not unless the Talent happens to be a hypnotist, no."

Looking into those dark eyes was tiring, Ania found. In them lay such intensity she couldn't bear it for long. He didn't need telepathy to tell her what he wanted. She laughed but it sounded high-pitched. "Are you never satisfied?"

"Not where you're concerned." His voice throbbed with desire.

She stepped back. She had to, just to get her breath. "What have you been doing the last two weeks?"

"Closing down a couple of labs, but not the main one we're looking for. We searched Jeanine's apartment and found some leads, but not to Bennett, at least not directly." He shoved his hands in his pockets and leaned against the wall outside her room. "Will you be long?"

"Doing what?"

"Packing. Do you need some help?"

She stopped and stared at him. "Pardon me?"

He waved at her to hurry her along. "To get your stuff together."

She shook her head. "I'm not going anywhere. You're welcome to stay if you want to, but I'm not leaving Andros on his own."

"He's a big boy and I don't think he's in any danger."

"Not from Bennett's people, perhaps, but try vampires."

Johann straightened up and she could have sworn his shoulders widened when he took his hands out of his pockets. "Okay," he said slowly. "Talk to me."

She went into her room, shoved a heap of clean laundry aside and sat. Johann chose to remain standing, just inside the door, but although he'd put his hands back in his pockets, he didn't look relaxed at all. From the shape of the material she could tell he'd fisted his hands.

"It's why I don't like vampires. The only ones I'd ever known about were leeches." Johann raised a brow but said nothing. He didn't need to. She spread her hands in a placatory gesture and carried on. "I told you he was ill. Andros' life is going to be shorter, his muscles will weaken and atrophy and he'll lose control. We don't know how long he has but he's getting worse. He tires easily, he can't concentrate some days and medicine can only do so much for him." She choked back her tears. They didn't help anyone and she'd cried enough about Andros.

Johann lifted his head to meet her eyes. She looked away. "Do you need more medical insurance?"

She shook her head. "No. We all got insurance and I've kept it up. Andros was insured before he was diagnosed, so the premiums were reasonable and before that we didn't know of any health problems in the family. Of course, with many of them losing their lives in the concentration camps we lost a lot of history. But we were—lucky, if you can call it that. My parents lived in a very large house in a great area. My mom's last illness took all our savings, but the sale of the house left us solvent." For the first time she realized what she'd lost. The effort of outlining her dilemma as concisely as she could brought it all into sharp perspective. Her parents had worked hard, made money with their house cleaning business, so by the time they sold up and took it easy they had a house as big as some of the ones they used to clean and money invested and in the bank.

Simply Service was an extension of that. From cleaning to catering, a fairly small step and at first a lucrative one. Enough so that when her mother fell ill Ania had trusted Sheila to take care of the day-to-day stuff.

Now she had nothing. Enough from the sale of the house to take care of Andros' medical bills. That was all. Even this apartment was rented. She had to stop her mind racing and stop fretting. But these days she found it harder and harder to concentrate. She made the effort and focused on Johann's fists, balled up tight in his pockets. She had no clue why he should be so wound up about this. She'd tell him and make it so he wasn't sorry for her. She was no charity case. They'd be okay, Ania and her brother.

Vampires, right. "We started looking at alternatives. They say that alternative medicine often helps chronic disease better than the regular type. We tried Chinese medicine, meditation, acupuncture, but Andros just got worse. Andros volunteered for experimental programs but they never offered us anything."

She swallowed and stared down at her clothes. A speck of white marred her navy skirt. Outside this apartment she was neat and precise. It was only home where she let herself go. She usually stripped out of her work clothes and stored them inside out to stop the dark fabrics collecting the fluff that seemed to gather in this place. She picked off the fluff and rolled it between her fingers. "Andros' band played a place called The Pit. Sheila got them the gig, she knew the manager. It's a hot club in town, restaurant by day, opens as a club at night. It's doing great business." She sighed. "When Talents came out last year, several members of the club came out too. Vampires. They turned it into some kind of Goth and Emo place where they hang out for food. Vampires give orgasms in return for food. Did you know that?"

When she looked up at him, he met her gaze blandly. "I kinda knew it, yeah. We push endorphins into the system, enough to give the—person a high."

"You were going to say 'prey,' weren't you?" That put her in her place. Prey.

He shrugged. "It's just a word. Like mortal and immortal. It doesn't really mean anything."

"It might to the prey. They promised Andros that they'd help him. If he converted, they said, he wouldn't be ill anymore. That true?"

She didn't imagine the spark of red that lit his eyes, like a light going on behind them, but it went again, faded. Maybe vampires weren't so dormant in the daytime. "As far as it goes, yes."

She sprang to her feet. "There's a catch, isn't there? I knew there was, I *told* him. Nobody gives up something for nothing. He said it was the blood, but he's getting worse. He gives blood every night and he's getting desperate."

Johann's eyes burned her, even though she looked away. "Let me get this right. They said they'd convert him if he fed them?"

"That's about it." She turned away to stare out the window. Not that the view was anything special, but it meant she didn't have to look at him. She still wanted him, he still turned her on and he shouldn't. He just shouldn't. She stared at the redbrick of the building opposite, another apartment building. "Does that mean they won't?"

"It's highly unlikely."

"Mind telling me why?"

She spun around to confront him and found him far closer than she'd thought. When she gasped, he caught her elbows. "I want you to promise me something."

"And you'll believe me without reading my mind?"

"Of course." And the way he said it, it sounded completely natural. The way things should be. "Promise me you won't tell anyone else what I'm about to tell you now. Whatever it is."

"I promise I won't tell."

"It's something vampires have decided not to make public for now. We'll decide, although someone might let it out one day. Let's not make it us."

He glanced out the window then led her away, toward the bed. He sat on a couple of sweaters and she sat on the bare spot of bed next to him. He kept hold of one of her hands and kept looking into her eyes.

"If they promised your brother conversion, they were lying. In order to convert a mortal to vampire, the sire has to give up his own life."

She pinched the bridge of her nose with her free hand. "I knew something was wrong. They've been stringing him along for a year now and he's no closer. His work is suffering because he's using all his energy on the band and the club. He does favors for them. I want him out of there."

"The band or the club?"

"The club. I think the other band members are doing it too. Hoping for conversion." She frowned. "Why don't you tell people?"

He took her other hand and stroked the palm with his thumb. "Can you imagine what would happen? It's too dangerous right now. We're trying to introduce knowledge gradually, roll it out because the law hasn't caught up with our existence yet. Nor will it for quite some time. They'll rush some ill-thought-up laws through, try to regularize us, and the Talented community won't stand for that. Conversion for us, for shape-shifters and others, is one of the secrets we're keeping for now." He watched her absorb his information. "The labs like to capture vampires, or they did. They'd starve their captive and then try to force the vampire to feed to death to watch the conversion. It happened a couple of times that I know of. The IRDC wanted to make money from Talents, to discover our secrets and use them." He hesitated and bit his lip, but went on after a moment. "They used the charity as a cover and sponsored the sleep clinics that Bennett ran. That was one of the ways they recruited people to use as test subjects. Afterward, they'd kill and dissect both the Talent and the converted one. They'd use sick people desperate for a cure and lie to them."

He stopped then. He didn't have to say any more. She understood more than she wanted to. She swallowed her distress. She needed to know, she needed to talk. Not cry. "Then Andros went to The Pit and he's been—donating, they call it. No harm investigating all the possibilities, he said. But there is harm, isn't there?"

Johann nodded. "Now I understand why you're averse to vampires. They're leeching off your brother." His mouth thinned and his eyes gained a hard look to them. "I'll make sure that's stopped. It isn't something the community approves of, but I've heard of a few of them recently. Clubs where vampires trade on the glamorous image they have to get easy prey."

"Can you get addicted to doing it? Giving blood, I mean?"

He shook his head and his lips relaxed a little. "Not hardly. We won't have to wean him away."

"He'll fight. He won't like it. He's getting desperate."

Slowly, he tugged on her hands and brought her closer until she rested in the circle of his arms, her head against his chest. "We'll sort it out."

"And then what?" Hopelessness swamped her, as it did sometimes. Even with someone, occasionally everything got on top of her and she felt she'd never get out of the hole she'd dug for herself. "Andros will still have MD."

"But he won't have other people using him. He can face what's ahead and try to accept it. There are no miracle cures, *miláčku*, there never are. People are looking for them again now that they know Talents exist, now that they know our lifespans are longer than the average mortal."

"How long?"

"What?" He kissed her forehead.

"If you tell me not to worry my little head about it, I'll throw you out now."

He chuckled. "No, I won't. Shape-shifters live for around five hundred years. Sorcerers have a mortal lifespan. And vampires are a little different. Our life expectations vary hugely, and we don't really have an average. At least, not one that matters. You want to know how old I am, don't you?"

She nodded, then shook her head. "Not now, not today. Let me think you're about thirty-five, at least for now. It's not as if we're a permanent fixture, is it?" Hurriedly, before he could reply to that, and the answer could only be "no", she went on. "We don't have to exchange all our deepest fears, do we?"

He didn't reply, not in words anyway. Just held her closer and gave her the comfort she so badly needed right now. They sat like that for an untold time except when she glanced at her bedside clock, the digits read 18:05. She glanced up to see him watching her. Outside, the sunlight was getting softer, less harsh. "You'll turn vampire soon, won't you?"

He nodded and lifted one hand to stroke her hair. "In about an hour. Do you mind or do you want me to leave?"

"Is there a way of telling?"

"Not with me. Sometimes people can tell, with fire in the eyes and maybe the fangs coming down, but you learn to control the changes. It becomes almost automatic. You want to watch me?"

She wet her lips. "I'm not sure. I don't know. No, don't go."

With a shock, she realized she was telling the truth. She didn't want him to go. Vampire or man, she felt safer with him around, loved that he told her the truth. So many lies all around her and she'd found someone who respected her enough to answer her questions truthfully, or just refuse to tell her. He'd trusted her with a secret. That meant a lot to her too. "So what do we do now?"

"When does your brother go to the club?"

"Almost every night. Around nine, if the band is playing. They play for an hour starting at ten, then break, then play for another hour. If he has classes the next day he comes home. They're his two priorities."

"And you're nowhere."

"No. He loves me."

He held her tighter. "But he takes you for granted. Assumes you'll look after the practical side of life."

"He's younger than I am and he has a lot to cope with."

He didn't reply immediately, but drew her back to rest on his chest again. The soft cotton of his shirt soothed her. Even more the body underneath. Hot, Johann felt hot. She thought vampires were supposed to be cold, chilly even. "Okay, so that gives us time. I'll make a few calls and arrange a personal visit to The Pit. We'll see what's going down and we'll take care of it if we have to. If the vampires who go to this place are lying in order to obtain blood, we can stop that and get your brother out of there."

She gave one long sigh.

"But I want something in return." She lifted her head to meet his gaze and he gazed back. As if he couldn't help himself, he pulled her up, met her halfway and kissed her. Their mouths met in a searing promise and he tasted her, only to draw away and kiss her from a different angle. One of his hands came up to cup the back of her head and hold her in place.

She would have given it all up then, given him anything he wanted, but the sound of the front door slamming made her jerk away. Before she could pull out of his arms she heard Andros' voice. "I'd say get a room, but you have one. You could close the door. Hi, stranger, my name's Andros. Didn't I see you earlier?"

Ania sat with her back to the door. Johann glanced up. "We've already met."

She heard Andros' whistle. "Well done, sis. I thought you were heading for the virgin record."

She chuckled weakly and sat up to face him. "I've not been a virgin for a while."

Her brother grinned back. "You might well have been for the last four years or so. About time. You want me to go away? Give me five dollars for the cinema and I'll get out of your hair."

"It'll cost more than that."

Andros' mouth twisted. "Not when you know as many film students as I do."

"So what do you study, Andros?"

"Music." Andros gave Johann a look that promised retribution if he hurt his sister. Ania had no inclination to laugh, even though Johann had twice Andros' muscle tone and probably overtopped him by half a head. "History as well as practical." He glanced at Ania. "I'm meeting someone at The Pit tonight. He says he knew Mozart. Of course, he might be spinning a yarn, but it's a hell of a lot more fun than a lot of the lies I hear."

He strolled away. "Shall I put some coffee on or are you closing that door?"

Johann got to his feet and crossed the room, dodging the pair of shoes that could have brought him to his knees. He glanced back at Ania, then grasped the knob and closed the door gently. "Unless you're desperate for coffee?" He quirked a brow.

She couldn't help it—she laughed. "I think I can wait."

He slid his hand into his pocket and drew out a slim cell phone. "Let me make those calls." His gaze lingered on her, and she heated as he smiled.

She'd never known phone calls could be erotic. All the time he spoke to Chase Maynord, he watched her, let his hot gaze caress her, almost as if he were touching her with his eyes. And it felt like that too.

Chapter Eight

** හ**

By the time Johann finished his call, Ania was trembling. Not with fear. Anticipation heated her blood. She couldn't believe he could heat her up just like that but by now she had to believe it was the sheer chemistry that sizzled between them, not any weird Talent influence. He was still a man, the sun was still up, but it didn't make any difference. When they'd fucked earlier today he'd been a man and he felt exactly as he had when he was vampire. Hot, warm, wanting. That was all she wanted. At least that was what she told herself, though her skin remembered his soft touches, the way his hand drifted over the curve of her waist and lingered, stroking softly. He liked that, she'd noticed him doing it more than once and it made her want to stretch and purr like a kitten.

No, she couldn't want more than she had. Remembering she was here and he was there, in New York, living his life, this couldn't work. And not forgetting that he was a vampire. And she hated vampires. Or she thought she did.

Right now a certain vampire was burning her up without even touching her. Although when he took the two careful strides that took him to her, avoiding the clutter on the floor, she heated just a bit more.

He lifted his hand to the side of her face, and stroked her, so softly she could have cried. Or screamed for him to catch hold. His voice came intimately, softly. "I want to read you this time, *zlatíčko*. Let me."

His touch mesmerized her, as did the endearment. "R-read me?"

"Your mind. Just the outer part, the part most people leave open. The part you've shut tight. Listen, whatever you say, I want you. But if I can read what you want, I can give it to you." He groaned. "Fuck, don't look at me like that. Ania, you're turning me inside out. I'll take you whatever, however, but I would like to read you. I miss it, that extra sensation."

She lifted her hand to cover his where it rested on her cheek, felt her loosened hair tickle the back of it. "I said no because I knew what you were. And because it scares me, this mind sharing. If I let you in, does that mean I let everyone in?"

He shook his head. "Not if you don't want it. I'm sorry, I shouldn't have asked. I should have respected your privacy."

Who knew vampires could be so considerate? Certainly not her. "Yes. The answer's yes. Read me. Just make me feel good, Johann." She needed that, especially today. For the last two weeks she'd missed him every day, although she hadn't wanted to. Found her mind wandering at inopportune moments, recalling their encounter. So now that she had him again, she'd make the most of him, however short their encounter.

Because if she ever forgot that, she'd hurt too badly to heal.

Johann glanced over her head and frowned. Ania grinned. "The bed, right?"

"How do you...?" His voice tailed off.

Ania shrugged. "Untidiness isn't important. The place is clean. There's just too much stuff, that's all. Push it on the floor."

His smile was one of the best things about him. She hadn't seen it often, but every time it enchanted her a little more. It made her a complete pushover.

Which was what he did. Gently pushed her until her knees hit the back of the bed, then eased her down and followed her, to lie over her, his legs straddling hers, his elbows on either side of her head. Surrounding her without touching her, but near enough that she felt his heat. His gaze met hers, so close she could count the sparks of fire in the dark pupils.

He bent his head, so slowly. She knew he was about to kiss her, but she watched and waited, the anticipation so delicious part of her wanted his approach to go on forever. She committed this moment to her memory. The way he looked, a slight smile tilting his finely cut lips, warmth filling his usually hard eyes. She'd remember all that forever.

When his lips touched hers she sighed in sheer happiness. Anticipation could be the best part, but in this case, it was only one part of the experience. And making love to Johann was a whole lot of experience.

He tilted his head a little and she willingly opened her mouth under his so he could enter and she could enter him. She lifted her arms to him slowly, so slowly, and slid them under his shirt, his skin hot and smooth to her touch. Goose bumps prickled up, evidence of his arousal, but not as potent as the hard bulge pressing against his pants. Her mouth watered. This time she wouldn't let him have it all his own way. Right now she was losing herself in his kiss and the feel of his body under her hands. He'd undone her blouse without her noticing. Not that she cared, until she felt his palms smoothing over her skin.

Magic happened right here in this room, the room she hated. She could learn to love it. Or to love him, except that wasn't allowed.

Just feel. Nothing else.

Muscles rippled under his skin as he moved, lifted slowly away from the kiss and glanced down to where his hand covered her breast. "I'll have to get you some pretty lingerie," he said. "You have a body that deserves celebrating."

"I'm sorry. I've been buying for comfort."

"I'm sure silk bras are very comfortable too." He touched his lips to the flesh above her sensible white bra. Perhaps losing interest in her body was part of the grieving process or perhaps she'd just been too busy. It seemed easier to grab the brand she knew fit her instead of lingering in front of a mirror trying something more elaborate in silk and lace. She wore stockings because bare legs weren't professional-looking and she hated pantyhose. But she was glad of that now when he slid his hand down her body, his big palm encompassing her stomach, stroking over her pubis to caress the skin between stocking top and panties. He unclipped the stockings and glanced away from her for long enough to drag them off, unzip her skirt and get that off too.

He stood to undress, stumbling slightly on some obstacle she couldn't see, and watching him, she stripped too, heedless of where her clothes fell.

Leaning forward, he pressed a kiss to her stomach. "We shouldn't be this hungry for each other, but I want you as if I hadn't already had you once today. I want you so bad."

"Me too." She licked her lips, suddenly gone dry. Especially when she heard him breathe deeply, taking in her essence and sighing in pleasure. "That's good. You smell good."

The sun filtered through the window, mellow now, a golden ball on its way down, but she felt a quiver in his skin, a tightening of his muscles. "Does it hurt?"

"What?"

"When you turn vampire?"

He chuckled, his breath tickling her stomach. "No. It's more of an awareness. And some exhilaration. But nothing as good as this."

"That's ridiculous. You can't compare doing something as ordinary as sex to doing something most of us relegated to the storybooks. Only it's not a story."

He licked her skin, making a sound of appreciation. "Mmm. It's ordinary to me and has been for most of my life. This, this now, is the most extraordinary thing. You're like no other woman, Ania. Ania." He repeated her name, rolling his tongue around the soft "n", as if tasting it. Then he tasted her and she leaned back against the covers, clearing the bed with one sweep of her arm and ignoring the thumps and bumps as various articles fell to the floor. Later.

He opened her with his thumbs and air hit her overheated skin, making her shiver in response. She glanced down to see him staring at her with unconcealed delight and hunger. With a soft sigh of pleasure, he leaned forward and licked her, one long savoring taste from opening to clit.

Then he stopped at her clit and sucked it in, pulling hard, and she clapped her hand over her mouth before she shrieked aloud and brought her brother running, although she hoped he'd have the sense not to. Still, she didn't want him eavesdropping, however unwittingly, on what they were doing.

Or what Johann was doing. He released her clit only to suck it in again, hard and deep, and no sooner had her libido screamed into overdrive than he released it again. His forefingers slid down her inner crease, his thumbs on the outside of her labia, pinching lightly and opening her wide so he could taste every part of her.

Then she felt him in her mind. A warm tingle but not unpleasant, like the shot of electric current.

That feel good?

The contact was so intimate, both mind and body, that she moaned his name, feeling his tongue delve inside her, then return to curl around her clit and tease it, arousing it even more.

Answer me, miláčku. Like this.

I can't. I don't know how.

Chuckling low in his throat, he returned to his task, his job done. Wonder filled her when she realized she'd spoken to him telepathically. She'd never done that before, presuming she needed special training. Not that and certainly not this.

Owning her, possessing her like this, he could do anything he wanted, ask anything he wanted. If only he'd make her come. He worked her, easing off when she thought she'd have to come, so he had her begging him. If anyone had asked her if she cared about her brother hearing, she'd have asked, "Who?" because nothing mattered now except that one thing, tingles suffusing every part of her body.

So pretty. That's right, plead with me and I might make you come.

You can't stop me.

Oh yeah? He backed off again for what seemed like the hundredth time and she howled in frustration. "No, no, please, Johann, please let me come!"

If you insist.

With one slurp, he sent her into a howling frenzy. Little explosions all over her body combined to make one big, roaring orgasm and Ania cried out and clutched at the empty space above her.

Then it wasn't empty anymore but filled with hard, determined male. A male who entered her in one devastating thrust so when she finally stopped quivering, he was moaning. He laid his head next to hers and murmured softly to her. When she came to a little bit, she realized he was speaking Czech, his native tongue. It sounded beautiful to her and once she picked up the cadence and his accent, she recognized a paean of soft compliments and soothing murmurs. She only knew a few words, but the sound was similar to Polish, which she knew. The familiar sounds sent her up again, so although she'd imagined giving him her attention now, he was still in control. And she loved it.

Nothing soft about the hard cock now tunneling inside her though. She closed her eyes and tightened her vaginal muscles just to feel him and listened to his responsive moans. He switched to English. "Do that much more and we won't be having dessert."

"You're f-feeding me as well?"

He thrust deep inside her. "This is the main course. Hungry for more?"

"Yes!"

Johann took her on the wildest gourmet tour she'd ever had. Hard thrusts, his mind still in hers, not speaking in words but sending images, of places and things she'd never seen. But he had. The Northern Lights, a close-up of a volcano, the way a bird swooped over the land, and she knew she was no match for him.

Though it didn't stop her trying after he'd taken her up again on another wild, mindless orgasm.

Despite the aircon, which she preferred to crank up, they were both sweating when he paused and ran his hand over her slick body, a slight tremble telling her he'd had to exert a lot of self-control to prevent himself joining her this time.

She lay panting under him, staring straight into his eyes. The sparks were more than in evidence now, flaring like tiny bonfires in the darkness of his irises, his teeth bared as he laughed in sheer joy. She felt the joy, he shared it with her, took from her and gave her his. "I want time to stop. Right now, just stop so we can stay here."

"I promised you dessert." He kissed her, took her mouth in savage possession before he reared back and exposed her upper body to the air. A chill breeze blew between them and she sighed in delight and squirmed to take advantage of it. Inside her, she felt him tighten.

When he withdrew from her body she whimpered, but didn't have time to do any more before he sat up and took her hands, dragging her upright. His cock glistened with their juices, inviting her to taste. She badly wanted to know what they tasted like together, and she wondered at something she'd considered unpleasant before she'd met and known Johann.

He didn't give her a chance. As she sat, he grasped her waist, lifted her and brought her down again, impaling her to her core. She lifted her hands and almost by accident found his shoulders, holding on while he brought her down. He sat, his legs curled behind her, supporting her, and she straddled him, his cock embedded deep inside her.

Another time, miláček. *You can taste me while I'm tasting you, afterward, so we both know what we taste like. But I don't want to come in your mouth now and if you did that to me, I'd be there. I want to give you more of this.*

Miláček. Polish for "darling". It sounded precious, better than when anyone else spoke the language. She loved it, the endearment, so carefully used. Smiling, she kissed him, but instead of the ravaging taking of a few moments ago, gentled it, added tenderness and received tenderness in return.

She lifted and glided down his cock, feeling her juices lubricate them both, making it easy to take him and work him, but she kept it gentle and controlled. He helped, guiding her, and then he angled her back a little more. Still in her mind, they both felt the jolt when he touched her sweet spot, deep inside. "That's it. Go there. Take me with you."

She worked him. Every time she sank down she had her reward, his cock head caressing that spot, so ultra sensitive her initial instinct was to squirm away but he held her firm, made her hit that spot again and again. "Take it just right. Just how you want it," he murmured and without changing the angle of his entry, leaned forward to take a nipple delicately between his teeth, nipping sharply. Her gentle cry followed and he licked her, sucking the tip into his mouth and stroking her with his tongue before taking the nipple right inside and sucking hard for a brief moment. Echoing and enhancing the sensations lower down, he drove her to a different kind of high where she remained in control. He guided her down, but if she'd moved he wouldn't have prevented her. Stroke by stroke her sensitivity rose, the stimulation working her up and up, toward a climax that wasn't the fiery, uncontrollable surge of the previous one, but a celebration. A soft patter of fireworks over water, ethereal, beautiful and almost unbearable in its intensity.

This time he joined her. He released her breast and dropped his forehead against her shoulder. Hardly moving now, she felt his series of sharp jerks, and in her head the lightning bolts of his orgasm. Inside, his honey bathed her womb in sweet sustenance. He expelled his breath in one long sigh, barely making a sound.

The only sound in the room was their soft breathing and the whirr of the aircon unit, creating a breeze around them. As peaceful as a light wind in the desert.

Until a shriek outside, high pitched but undoubtedly masculine, roused them.

Chapter Nine

✌

Someone hammered on her door and Johann lifted his head. It felt heavier than he could remember, but he forced himself into awareness. He'd kill the little fucker when he got out of here. Then he heard what Andros was actually saying and noticed the little wisps of mist coming under the door.

"Get out now! Somebody threw a bomb through the window!"

Why hadn't he heard glass shattering? Heat. The idiot had opened a window. Jesus.

Johann tried to think, forced his brain into working again.

Glass splintered, a sound he hated, and something black sailed into the room. He didn't know what it was but it wouldn't be anything good. He rolled out of bed, pushing Ania in front of him so they both landed on the floor on the opposite side of the object. Only just in time. A sheet of flame temporarily blinded him and he did what his instincts told him to do.

He flashed them out of there. Ania's scream, begun in her apartment, ended in his hotel suite.

She grabbed him, eyes wide and scared. "What was it? Where's Andros?"

"Shit. Wait here."

He went back, praying the room was still there, otherwise the transfer would kill him. Flashing, or instantaneous transfer, as some pedants had it, was fucking dangerous in these circumstances but he had no choice.

The room was one sheet of flame and Johann landed in the pocket of air under the bed. He caught his breath and rolled out, not stopping, heading for the door.

It burst open under his shoulder and he cannoned into Andros, lying on the floor with his clothes on fire. He moved fast, flashed and they both landed on the floor of his bedroom in his suite. He rose to his knees, then grabbed Andros and rolled with him to douse the remaining flames. He wasn't left with many clothes after that.

Ania gasped. Johann sent out a fast message. No time for niceties, he broadcast to any Talent in the vicinity.

Then he sat back, panting, trying to make sense of what had just happened. Oh yes, he had it now. He got to his feet just as the outer door to the suite opened and Chase and Jack rushed in.

Johann closed the bedroom door behind Ania and her brother and faced his colleagues. "Ania's apartment was firebombed. Is being firebombed. No doubt they wanted them dead. It was a take-no-prisoners attack."

"Fuck!" Chase closed his eyes and Johann knew he was projecting. "Okay, I'm sending a team in. We need to know who and why." He opened his eyes again, focused on Johann. "So what do you think?"

"I was busy, but not too busy to stay on guard." He grimaced. "I didn't get any warning, which in itself is a sign. Anyone planning to firebomb an apartment would be agitated or excited and I didn't pick any of that up in the immediate vicinity. But I was—busy at the time, so don't take that as absolute."

"The labs or the IRDC then," Chase said grimly.

Johann crossed the room, heading for the windows. He flicked the blinds closed before he turned on more lights and spotted a pair of his jeans. He picked them up and climbed into them. Neither of his companions commented. Shape-shifters like Jack were used to others seeing them naked, and even though he was relatively new, Jack had adapted to the life easily. Chase had been around Talents for most of his life. Johann just didn't give a fuck. "We need to act before they attack again."

Jack frowned, his dark brows snapping together over his dark eyes. "So what do you want to do about it, Johann?"

"We'll go for The Pit. It's our only lead."

Jack grinned. "Sounds like fun. Count me in. Maybe a jaguar shape-shifter running riot in their precious club will knock them into next week."

Chase sent him a scornful look. "Fuck, you're so British sometimes."

Unabashed, Jack grinned. "Yep."

Johann crossed the room. He'd kept his mind locked with Ania, now that she'd permitted it, and he had no intention of letting go until he was certain of her safety. He wouldn't leave her for a minute now. Before he went back into the bedroom, he faced the other two. "We'll go in undercover, get Andros to take us in as mortals, see what crawls out from under the stones when we turn them over. But we need to take that place down."

He cocked a brow toward Jack, who nodded and gave him a terse, "Call me."

Chase gave a sharp nod. "Okay. Jillian will kill me if she finds out, or should I say *when* she finds out, but I can't let you go in alone. Besides, it could be fun." And this time his grin did hold some humor.

Johann wanted to get back to Ania. "Let me know what you find out about the firebombing. Meanwhile I have a distressed woman to soothe and her brother is more agitated than he's letting on. He can sleep on the couch tonight, but we need to get a few things straight in the morning."

"I'll find a room for him. And I'll have some things sent up for them."

Johann paused, his hand on his bedroom door. "Oh shit. She won't have anything left, will she?" All those things she wanted to keep, the books, the boxes full of her life, the clothes. All gone.

"I'll get the boutique to send clothes, toiletries and makeup. And a credit card, though I don't want her going out tomorrow. She can shop online."

Johann lifted his hand in a vague gesture. "Whatever. And thanks for the help."

"Do you know her size?"

He shrugged. "Only that she's curved in all the right places."

He squared his shoulders and went through to the woman he was fast coming to regard as his own.

* * * * *

Landing in a hotel room stark naked, only to have your brother, naked except for his boxers and some charred rags, landing next to you a moment later wasn't Ania's ideal way of waking after what had proved to be some of the best sex of her life. Rude awakening didn't begin to describe it.

Ania scrambled into the big bed and sat up, drawing the covers around her, and went back over what seemed to be the last five minutes. She checked the bedside clock. Fifteen minutes.

Something had caught fire and Johann had gotten her and Andros out of there. Apart from that she had no clue.

Andros, sitting on the floor with his elbows propped on his upraised knees and his head sunk between his hands, groaned. "You okay, sis?"

"I think so. Yes. I'm fine. Do you think you could find us bathrobes or something?"

Andros hauled himself to his feet and opened a door at random. It proved to be a large closet with a good selection of male clothing. "This do?" He grabbed a shirt off the nearest rail and tossed it to her. She glanced at it and put it aside. "If you can't find a robe. But it's an evening shirt, too starchy for me. I'll wear the sheet instead." She tugged at the sheet and while Andros was engaged in getting into a pair of jeans he'd snagged, she got off the bed and draped the sheet around her, toga style. Unfortunately there was masses of sheet, it being a big bed, and she ended with a lot of it trailing behind her. Since it was fine cotton, not silk, bunching wasn't a big help. But at least she wasn't naked anymore. She and Andros had given that up when he was around two years old and stopped sharing a bath.

Sometimes she felt much more than four years older than her brother, and this was one of the times. She had started to take a heavy-hearted mental inventory of what she'd lost in the fire and he was intent on blatant admiration of Johann's clothes and the labels they bore. "Come out of there, Andros. I'm sure Johann doesn't want you pawing through his clothes."

Andros came out of the walk-in, scowling. "I was only looking. Which reminds me. Mind if I have the first shower?"

She looked at the soot adorning his face and his decidedly tousled hair and remembered what she still had instead of what she'd lost. "Go ahead. Johann had me out of the apartment before the fire really touched me."

"Oh yeah." Andros opened a door that led to a bathroom and turned back. "You never told me your new boyfriend was a Talent. And the way he got us out of there tends to indicate he's a vampire. If that was for me, thanks. But I'm sorting that side of it out for myself."

He left her alone. She heard the spray as he turned on the shower and she sat on the bed, her mind returning to the apartment. Perhaps it was on TV? There was a small flat-screen on a table in the corner of the room, so she turned it on and found the remote, switching to one of the local channels.

Oh yes, there it was. Live pictures of the fire department spraying foam into the flames. The only way she recognized it was from the neighboring buildings. Her building was engulfed in flames.

She didn't turn around when the outer door opened. She knew from the touch in her mind that it was Johann. Strange how soon she could get used to it, going from fear of mental contact to acceptance in the blink of an eye. It didn't seem so important anymore. His hands clasped her shoulders and he sank down to join her where she sat on the thick rug covering this part of the floor. "I'm sorry."

"Who did it? Who would want to do such a thing?" She scanned the crowd as the camera panned over the onlookers and caught sight of a few of her neighbors. They'd lost their possessions too. She hoped they were insured. Her contents insurance would cover most things, and in a way it was lucky the fire had happened now because she didn't think she'd be able to afford the premium due next month. But nothing covered the precious photographs of her parents and the other personal tokens she'd moved into the cluttered space because she wanted to cling to a happier past. All gone now. With her clothes.

"We think it's the labs, but it could be the vampires from The Pit if Andros has upset them enough. Or the IRDC, for some reason. Chase is looking into it."

"It's all gone. What the fire didn't get, that foam will." She stared at the screen, willing it not to be real. She'd wake up in a minute.

Idiot. This was it, now.

She felt his arms wrap warmly around her. His chest was bare, as was the top of her back and her shoulders, and she relaxed into the intimacy. Somehow it had become easy to relax with Johann, and her big bad vampire had become a rounded person. "Chase is getting some racks of clothes sent up for you. Choose whatever you want."

She sighed in relief that something at least was being taken care of. One less thing to worry about although she didn't feel particularly relieved. Just slightly less worried. Although she kept telling herself that her brother was alive and unhurt and she was too, her mind kept taking inventory of everything she'd lost.

Leaning against Johann's hard warmth soothed her and gave her the illusion of safety. Because now she knew it had to be an illusion. Nobody was safe, anytime, anywhere. She shivered and his arms closed around her. He pressed a kiss to her neck. "I promise, Ania, you're safe with me. I'll do my best to protect you, to take care of you. That's all I can do."

"I know and I appreciate it. But I have to learn to do this on my own. I learned early on that nobody can shelter you, and even if they could you wouldn't want them to."

The picture on the TV changed to a local politician making a speech. She turned the sound up a little, but it wasn't anything about the fire, so she switched off and dropped the remote.

Too tired to think, too upset to work out her next move, she curled into him, seeking warmth and shelter. Behind them a door opened but she took no notice. "Hey you two, get a room," she heard from her brother. The second time in the same day. She smiled.

Johann spoke quietly, but nobody could have misheard him. "In case you didn't notice, I do have a room and this is it. Chase is finding you another room on this floor, Andros. You and your sister have to stay here. You're in the Timothy hotel on a secure floor and you won't be able to leave without our permission. But you'll be comfortable. Relax, go to bed and sleep. I'll take care of your sister."

"I need some meds."

Ania heard the edge in Andros' voice and tried to turn in Johann's arms, but he held her firmly. "He takes several pills every day and he has more of others in case he needs them."

"We know. Tell the guard outside what you need and we'll get it for you. The doctor who visits sick guests here will see you in the morning and prescribe a supply of your meds. Chase is on it."

Andros grunted. "I need to call college. Tell them what happened."

"No problem. Just pick up the phone and ask for an outside line. Don't tell them where you are, just call in sick. But not until tomorrow, okay?"

Johann got to his feet, lifting Ania with him in a seemingly tireless effort, but she was in his mind now and she felt his weariness. Didn't he say that flashing was exhausting? And she wanted not to think now, just to curl up with him in the nearest bed and sleep. "Stay with me, Johann."

"All night. Chase and Jack are on the case. All we need to do is rest." He crossed the room to the bed and lowered her gently on to it. A movement to her left told her Andros was still in the room. She opened heavy lids to see him staring down at her. "You going to be all right, sis?"

She managed a smile, but only just. "Sure. Let's sleep now and worry about it in the morning. Until they put out the fire we can't assess the damage, and there isn't anything else we can do."

Andros lifted the towel in his hand and scrubbed his hair. It gleamed black in the bright light of the central light fitting. She squinted at him. Now that he'd showered she could see he wasn't hurt. A bruise marred the pale skin of his upper ribs and a couple of cuts, but apart from that he looked okay. She turned her head to see Johann, now sitting on the bed next to her. "You must have got us out fast."

His mouth flattened. "If I hadn't been there, you'd both have died. I guess Chase will come up with a story." He hit his forehead with the flat of his hand. "I forget. For years that came naturally to us, to cover up what we are and what we can do. Now we can say a Talent got you out. Shit, that's sick."

Andros grinned. "And you're a vampire, aren't you? I go all over town looking for Talents and she just happens on you. So can you help me?"

Johann lifted his gaze and met Andros' eyes. Neither man looked away, but because she was in his mind now, Ania could tell they weren't communicating telepathically. Just exchanging stares, as men have done since the first caveman found another stealing his deer.

"I'll tell you the truth. But you can't tell anyone else, not yet." Johann lifted his head but it was Andros who broke eye contact.

"Okay. I guess. My friends at The Pit told me a few secrets too. Like how conversion will cure my Becker's." He huffed. "It better, because nothing else will."

"Sit down, Andros." Johann glanced at Ania and this time spoke to her telepathically. *Stay. He might need you.*

Of course. She'd spoken before she thought about it. Shocked how easy she found it, she took a seat on the sofa where Johann had settled himself, but she didn't touch him. She kept her attention on her brother, not sure how he'd handle what Johann was about to tell him.

Johann crossed one ankle over his knee. "Yes, I'm a vampire. A vampire born. Converted vampires are rare, but I think your new friends have led you to believe otherwise."

"I met a couple of converts."

Johann rumbled low in his throat and Ania felt his anger. He was sharing that with her. She forced herself not to look at him. If Andros knew they were together mentally, this whole talk would be more difficult. "That's unlikely, but they could have found a few. You can't tell the difference. Once a vampire is converted, he or she is the same as any other. Poor fertility, the need to take blood, the longer lifespan and the occasional weird sensitivity are all part of the deal. And we don't discriminate either. They probably gave you all the junk about that."

He had Andros' attention, Ania saw the heightened awareness in the way her brother's body tensed and his fingers, relaxed on his knee, tightened a little bit. Andros jerked a nod. "They said I would have to be tested."

"And you say Sheila introduced you to the club and these people?"

"We dated for a while." He grimaced. "Older woman and all that. She's four years older than me. Was." A shadow crossed his eyes. Although she had a lot to condemn Sheila for, Ania was glad her brother could feel sorrow for a woman he'd been involved with.

Johann frowned. *There's something else there, something I'm missing.*

I know. But I have no idea what it is.

Johann shook his head and continued to talk to Andros, keeping his tone low and measured. "Vampires live a long time and they are extra strong. During the day they only have telepathy and maybe, if they're lucky, one or two other gifts. They can eat and drink normally. When the sun goes down, their metabolism changes. They can imbibe only blood, anything else makes them sick. The toothbuds that hold the fangs become active. And they—we—can convert a mortal to vampire." His mouth hardened and Andros leaned forward in his seat, his eagerness palpable. Ania hurt for him so much but he had to face this on his own. Johann continued, his implacable, quiet tones filling the tense space. "But a vampire can only convert a mortal at the expense of his own life."

Andros blinked, his mouth opened. "That can't be right—"

"It is. It's the only way a mortal can be converted to vampire. The vampire drains the mortal completely, and when the last drop leaves his body, the mortal is possessed with blood fever. He attacks the vampire, the fangs appear and he takes the vampire's blood. Every drop. And the vampire dies, leaving a newly made vampire in his stead. That's what happens. I can provide you with proof, if you want it." With a shock, Ania realized she'd accepted Johann's word for it without any proof. But he'd let her into his mind and she knew he wasn't lying.

Andros swallowed. "Why should I believe you?"

"Because I have nothing to gain or lose by telling you the truth, except that I'll stop you making a mistake."

Andros dropped his head between his hands. Ania had never seen him so despondent. Her brother kept his cool at all times, but this information had overwhelmed him. "Why would they tell me otherwise?"

"They're playing with you. Vampires aren't a homogenous type, our makeup doesn't mean we think and behave the same. These vampires are fucking with your head, probably to get easy blood. They fed on you and they're weakening you, but they don't care. Soon your disease will take you because you'll have squandered all your resistance on donating blood to bastards who don't deserve it. They won't help you, though I can introduce you to some people who might. No promises."

He lifted his head and the hope in his eyes made her realize that if Johann was lying to her, she'd kill him. Andros had been through enough. "And what do you want for that?"

"Nothing. Friends and family of Talents can join a list, a bit like the list for donating organs. Shape-shifters can convert one other person in their lives and sometimes, when they near death, if they haven't converted anyone, they'll donate their Talent. Vampires do that too. We all die, Andros, even if most Talents take much longer than mortals. And since Talents don't have the high fertility that mortals do, it's almost a duty. I have to say that finding a donor is tough, as tough as finding a donor heart when you need one, but at least it's on the level. And I should tell you that this is also something we're keeping to ourselves for the time being, until we can put a legal system in place, but we have agreed that people already on the list have priority, even when it becomes public. There'll be a rush, you know that. So many mortals want to convert."

"Family?" Andros glanced at Ania.

Johann sighed. "Something like that. I have a relationship with your sister, you know that too. As far as I'm concerned it's more than casual."

Shock arced through Ania and she turned to him, one hand lifting in protest. Johann moved fast, taking her hand and threading his fingers between hers. Her hand clasped in his, he brought them to rest on the cushions. Andros watched, fascinated, and Ania felt numb. "You can't mean that."

He didn't look at her. "We'll work something out." If only it were that easy. "So how about it, Andros? Do you want a shot at the real list?"

"Yes, of course I do!"

"I'll give you every opportunity to verify it for yourself."

"And what do I have to do in return?"

"Ah." He nodded. "Yes, I do intend to ask something. We intend to raid The Pit and put a stop to its activities. We in this case being STORM. So we want you to tell us all you know. The identities of the people there, how Sheila got involved in it, the layout of the place, everything."

Andros had come home one day saying he'd met a real live vampire. Talents were still exotic, distant beings to most people, they didn't announce themselves and they knew how to shield themselves telepathically. He'd dated Sheila a couple of times and she'd introduced him to a friend she'd claimed she only discovered recently was a vampire.

Andros shrugged. "What do I have to lose? All my clothes, my music, my laptop—just as well I use the university's backup system or all my essays and shit would have gone up with it. All gone. And my life, pretty soon." He faced Ania, his eyes grave. "They said it's getting worse, sis. That's what I didn't tell you the other day. Progress isn't something they can forecast, they said. It does what it does. And maybe all the blood donations weren't helping. They didn't say. Yes, I did tell them." His attention went to Johann, as if he couldn't bear to look at her anymore. "So yeah, if you can prove to me that you're the shit, I'll do it. For all I know they firebombed the apartment. Or you did. Or the IRDC did. If they'd killed Ania, I wouldn't have died until I'd seen them suffer, whoever they are." He pushed back the heavy fall of hair that usually hid half his face. His blond roots were beginning to show, gleaming in the low light. "So you take care of her, you hear? That's my condition. Look after her, be straight with her and I'll tell you everything I know."

He straightened and walked to the door. "I'm going to find Chase and tell him what we discussed. And I'll ask him to find me a room right now. You'll need your privacy when she starts throwing things at you."

She stared at the door as it closed behind her brother, outrage warring with astonishment in her mind. Johann tugged on her hand and only then did she remember she still gripped it. He pulled her closer and she lifted a little so she could comply. Velvet cushions didn't allow her to get closer without that.

"What are you talking about, a relationship?" She couldn't allow herself to believe it. "You live in New York, you hate LA and I can't leave, at least not until Andros finishes his studies."

"He's about to take his final exams. He doesn't have to hang around after that."

Ania had the irrational desire to hit him. "LA is my home."

"If you like, I'll move here. We have STORM agencies all over the States—all over the world, if truth be told. Admit it, Ania. There's something between us, something special."

"It's just sex." It was for him, anyway. At least she was almost sure of that.

"No, *miláčku*, it's not. If you lived as long as me, you'd know how rare this is. I want to tell you things you might not be ready for yet." He lifted their joined hands to his lips and

113

kissed the knuckle of her forefinger. His tongue came out and touched her skin. Ania shuddered and he gave her a slow smile kindling heat deep inside her. "See? It's more than sex, much more. I want to find out how much more and I think it's worth making an effort to find out. Distance is nothing, moving is nothing. Before Talents came out, I used to move continents when I switched identities. I could leave nothing behind. If I'd had a partner, we would be together, even if we had to spend time apart."

"Have you had a partner before?"

He watched her and kissed the next knuckle, lingering over it a little longer this time. "Not like this. I never felt this way before."

"Infatuation—a crush," she choked out.

"No. I've had those and I know the difference. And do you want to know the moment I realized we had more than sex? That we had something worth working on?" When she shook her head, he kissed the third knuckle. She relaxed her hold on him, a hold she hadn't been aware of before.

Johann smiled, one corner of his mouth kicking up in the way that made her heart twist. "When you let me into your mind this afternoon. I only read the surface, just as I promised, but it was enough. I felt at home, as if I'd entered somewhere I belonged. I don't belong, Ania, I've never belonged. Before this I loved being the loner, having no ties. It was a way of life that suited me. Had I been born mortal, I think I would have felt the same, but being a Talent in a world that didn't believe in us concentrated that. Now I'm ready. I'm not so devoted to my way of life that I won't change it if I find something better. And I have found something better. In you."

"No!" Her voice came out in a sob. It couldn't be right, to feel this bubble of happiness rising inside her. She'd lost her dearest belongings that night, together with her records. Her birth certificate, her records, her clothes. Her business was in shreds and she'd be lucky not to find herself in debt or even bankrupt when it was all worked out. And yet she felt happy, content as she'd never felt before. Settled. A strange feeling she wasn't at all sure she liked. Especially considering the circumstances. No home, no clothes, no money, nothing.

But he wouldn't let her deny it. "Yes." He caught her chin, forcing her to look at him. "Read the truth in me."

"You mean you I—"

Before she could finish he interrupted her. "No, not yet. Don't use the L word yet. It brings too much baggage with it. Let's accept we're together and go from there."

Disappointment warred with relief. At least he didn't want her to make that kind of commitment. How could she on a few weeks' acquaintance? What if he was a neatnik who couldn't bear her untidy ways? Andros had his own room—or used to have. Her mind began to run along rails that had become familiar in the last few hours. But he stopped that too by lowering his mouth to hers.

This time his kiss gave her soothing respite, taking her into his world. When she felt the first strokes in her mind, she almost purred. She'd never, never felt anything like it, as if he stroked her mind with a velvet cloth, and she very much feared it could be addictive. Instantly addictive. He drew his mouth away, his lips curving, his dark eyes filled with soft pleasure. "Come and bathe. Let's get one good night's sleep before it all starts all over again."

"Will—will he be all right?"

"Who?" Johann drew back, frowning, then his face cleared. "Andros? Jack will keep an eye on him. If I know Chase, he'll put them in the same suite. Don't worry, *láska*. Let me look after you now."

She was too tired to do anything else. Johann took her to the bathroom and she gaped. He hadn't taken her to this suite before, but another, more modest suite on another floor. He hadn't known her properly then and this was a secure floor. The place was larger than her living room, and she'd bought the apartment for the size of the main living space. A large half-sunken tub dominated the bathroom with a walk-in shower to one side, separated from the main space by a tiled half-wall. It was more like a luxury room in one of the mansions in Beverly Hills. But she knew better than to comment on it, instead pasting on a disinterested face.

Johann chuckled. "You forget, *miláčku*, I'm in your head. But you're not alone. When I first arrived in the States, their bathrooms exceeded anything I'd ever seen before."

"When was that? After World War Two?"

He gazed at her, his familiar smile curving his lips. "I'd visited before. But I don't think I'll tell you. Not yet, anyway. We have enough to cope with right now. Another time, later. Age doesn't mean the same thing to us. When your parents look younger than you do without plastic surgery, you tend to get a different perspective."

He flicked a switch on the wall and water poured into the deep tub like a waterfall. At this rate it wouldn't take long to fill. Johann stripped off the sheet she'd wrapped herself in and removed his jeans faster than she would have thought possible. He lifted her off her feet and took her into the bath. He reached for a jar, opened it and took an experimental sniff. "Don't want it too fou-fou," he explained before he tipped bath confetti into the water. Some of it stuck to her skin and she watched it dissolve as the water deepened. She seemed to have lost all her will. Johann put down the jar and reached for her, turning her in the water and pulling her against his chest. She nestled back against him, relishing the warmth seeping through her.

"Have you done anything to me?"

"What do you mean?" He kissed the top of her head.

"I don't seem capable of thought. Every time I try, everything skitters away."

"Skitters?" She couldn't see his face but she heard the smile in his voice. "No, I've done nothing. I won't, unless you want me to. That's another promise. But until you're out of danger, I won't leave your mind."

"I'm not sure I like that."

He curved his arm around her, holding her safe and close, his forearm supporting her breasts. "I'll just touch your mind. I need to know you're safe, Ania. *Need* it. I can't work properly if I'm not sure of it."

"Then can I read you?"

"Anytime, *miláčku*. Anytime."

He bathed her, using an oversize sponge, the slight roughness abrading her skin in direct contrast to the water, made silky by the bath confetti. She relaxed in his arms, occasionally asking desultory questions, knowing now that her exhaustion was all her own and she needed the rest before she could function properly again.

He washed her, lifted her out of the water and dried her with a big, soft towel. "Don't think of anything, not now," he said. "We'll rest. If I'm gone when you wake, just reach for me with your mind and I'll be there."

He patted her back dry and took her across the room to a cabinet, which he opened to reveal intriguing pots and containers. Full-sized, she noted, not the tiny bottles she was used to in hotels.

He took down a pot and smiled. "Body butter. Lemongrass and peach. Should be nice."

Despite her exhaustion, Ania shuddered at the thought of Johann rubbing the scented cream on her body. He pulled her close for a gentle kiss, but she felt his insistent cock prod her stomach. Not as gentle as he pretended then.

"Maybe not." She didn't know if she could get used to the combination of verbal and mental communication he seemed to use naturally. "Come on. Let's get you into bed."

He wouldn't let her do a thing for herself. He even drew back the covers and lifted her onto the cool, fresh cotton sheets before he opened the pot of body butter and turned her onto her stomach to massage her back. He had her moaning in delight before he turned her over and started on her front. That was even better. After he massaged her breasts, cupping and rubbing them gently, he shaped her nipples with the tips of his fingers and thumbs, as if he was working clay, getting it to his satisfaction. "Perfect," he murmured. "Everything about you is perfect."

She couldn't conceal her snort of derision. He gave her a reproving frown. "For me, you are. Beautifully curved, small, so you make me feel like a god when I make love to you. And your skin is so beautifully soft, silky, that I could worship it all day."

Ania glanced down to where his cock strained for attention. "Do you want me to use the body butter on you?"

Resting his hands either side of her, he shook his head. "Not tonight. Tonight is for you."

He ran his hands down her body and collected another scoop of the cream, starting on her legs. She watched him dreamily. He began at her ankles and worked up, massaging each muscle thoroughly, turning her into one mass of sensation. She couldn't think for herself anymore, but she knew it was her exhaustion rather than anything more sinister. She had to trust someone or she'd go mad. She'd trust Johann. For now.

His movements slowed, became more deliberate as he worked his way up her legs until she was almost screaming with frustration. For all the relaxation he'd invoked, now she could think of only one thing—his body inside hers. Deep, deep inside.

He opened her sex with his thumbs, his hands gripping her thighs, and he looked. She watched him lick his lips and he leaned forward, tasting slowly, before he drew back and used his hands on her. His fingers, pinching her clit between finger and thumb, the way he'd shaped her nipples, sensitized her skin, so she felt the way his hair brushed her thighs when he angled his head to study her from a different angle, the firm grip he had on her pressing in, just short of bruising. Carefully he inserted one finger inside her and she sighed in wanting, smiling up at him. "Fuck me, Johann."

He kissed her once more, long and lingering, before he removed his hands and lifted himself over her body. "Not tonight, Ania. Tonight we make love." And when he entered her, he did it firmly but without hurry, pushing slowly inside her, making her feel every inch of him filling her, sure and strong.

She held him against her, the sprinkling of hair on his chest caressing her, stimulating her nipples, and he smiled down at her before he kissed her, as carefully as he'd entered her body.

This felt better than good. "I'm going to persuade you to come, not force it out of you," he whispered against her lips, his breath washing hotly over her cheek. "Relax and think of nothing but me, nothing but this. That's it. Oh yes, that's it." He stroked her inside again, her pussy and her mind, and instead of immediately shooting up into a mind-blowing climax, she felt every moment of her arousal, every rung on the ladder to the top. Because he made sure she did. Occasionally he paused and waited for her to catch up to him, moving inside her, rotating his hips to touch every part of her deep inside. To her surprise she discovered that she had different sensations, different levels of sensation there. And all the time he watched her and she watched him and he had that elusive, slight smile on his beautiful lips, making her feel like the best, the most important person in the world. He bent and touched his lips to hers. "Right now, you are. More essential than anyone else."

She smiled back and felt herself melt around him. Her orgasm wasn't a surprise, but something worked for and won, and when the muscles of her pussy convulsed around his cock, she felt every tightening, every clench and release. And she watched him, felt the vein on the underside of his penis swell as his seed pulsed through and spurted inside her.

Johann clenched his teeth and his eyes widened before they closed in his instant of ecstasy. Sweat broke out on his forehead and he slumped forward, pressing Ania into the mattress.

She loved it. She was very much afraid that she loved him.

Chapter Ten

ᔓ

They rose late the next day and ate in their room. Ania itched to see her brother again, so much that she used the hotel phone to talk to him. He told her he was fine, that Jack was great, if a little angry, and the guy was a complete research freak. Ania heard with some incredulity that Jack had been an archivist before being recruited by STORM. Anyone less like a librarian she couldn't imagine, but she knew herself guilty of typecasting and absorbed the fact that Andros was dealing with this a lot better than she was.

At noon several beefy bellboys wheeled racks of clothes into the large living room in the suite, followed by boxes of lingerie. With a little encouragement from her lover, Ania lost herself in pleasure for the rest of the afternoon, but guiltily insisted that the most expensive items went back. Chase had made the mistake of leaving price tags on some of the items. Some items didn't have price tags but bore labels she knew she could never afford. But when she'd sorted through the delectable racks and tried a few of the more irresistible things on, she found herself left with a poor selection. It would do and her insurance would cover a couple of pairs of jeans, t-shirts, some of the plainer underwear and one good dress, because her mother had always insisted that one good dress was worth a dozen cheap ones. She put the other racks aside, ready for the staff to collect.

Johann claimed she looked tired. He took her into the bedroom and distracted her beautifully before leaving to meet with Chase and Jack. Relishing the crisp sheets, changed while they were in the bathroom that morning, Ania slid into sleep.

Only to discover that when she awoke, the small selection of plainer clothes had gone and only the most extravagant, filmy underwear remained and the clothes with labels but no price tags.

If she wanted to dress she had no choice, and deep inside a secret part of her rejoiced in the soft, silky feel of the garments, the way the jeans and t-shirt fit her so well, and when she turned to view her back in the mirror, the way the jeans clung to her butt, outlining every curve.

She found a brush and swept it through her hair. If only she could tame the frizz, she'd look pretty good.

She didn't turn when the door opened, but watched the mirror as Johann entered the room and closed the door quietly behind him. He leaned against it, and met her gaze. "Beautiful. Good enough to eat." A wicked gleam lit his dark eyes. "Again."

Mortified, she watched the flush mantle her cheeks. "You have to take these clothes back. I can't afford them."

He pushed away from the door. "I can." He crossed the room to her and took the brush from her unresisting hand. He smoothed her hair with one hand while he used the brush, flattening the frizz a little. "I love the feel of your hair on my naked skin. I can feel it in my sleep sometimes, so when I dream of the soft, warm sea of the Mediterranean, I know it's you." He paused. "I want you to have the clothes. I can't bear that desolate look you get when you think I'm not watching you. If I have anything to do with it, you won't feel desolate ever again."

"You can't know that."

"I can try." He put down the brush and rested his chin on the top of her head, gazing at her reflection. "Maybe I should let you know that I haven't been happy for a long time. No particular reason, just restlessness and a deep disappointment when Talents were outed. We used to explain the occasional appearance away, call it blimps, kites or just illusions. Even magic tricks. I liked it that way, even though I had to go through a fake dying and rebirthing process every so often. It was a small price to pay. We have legends and stories about dragons and vampires and nobody believed they were real. I liked that. Now we have journalists and politicians dragging their muddy feet through our lives, making the IRDC look almost clean." He grimaced. "I did say almost. I guess I didn't like change. I had my nice comfortable life and I wanted it to stay that way. I'd love to give you a tragic past or a secret sorrow, but I can't. It was simple unhappiness and depression. I just existed and the only emotion I felt was anger."

He curved his hands around her waist. "The first time I saw you, you brought something back to me. Dimly remembered emotions I hadn't known for a while. You moved through that crowd, smiling and dispensing drinks with a grace I hadn't seen for a long time. I almost forgot my mission, and considering one of my team members died pursuing Bennett and turned the operation personal, that's saying something. I wanted to follow you, not push after Jeanine. In that meeting just now, my mind drifted. Chase had to bring me back to the point a couple of times. I don't drift. I never miss the point." He kissed her hair. "But I did today, because I was thinking about you. So don't even try to pay for these things. Chase wanted to pay, but I want to do it. I want to see your ass cupped in those jeans, I want to know the shape of the panties under it."

"Thong," she said.

He groaned, making her smile. He made her feel powerful, though she knew anyone less than powerful would be hard to find right now. "Thong," he repeated, speaking slowly, savoring the word.

One aspect of this disturbed her. "You want to own me?"

"No." His immediate response went some way toward reassuring her. "I want to give you gifts occasionally, that's all. What you keep, what you throw away and what you buy for yourself are all your choice, but I can't deny it does turn me on to know you're wearing some of the gorgeous pieces of nothing I saw earlier today. I wanted to fuck you rigid, but I had to go to the meeting, so I thought about you modeling them for me instead." His gaze heated. "I still want that. Maybe we can call that payment. Deal?"

She knew when she was beaten. "Deal. So come and sit down and tell me what you decided." She paused. "And I want to know about your team member who died."

He stood back and took her hand to lead her to the sofa. They sat together on the big, squashy cushions and he put his arm around her shoulders. "Yeah. Well, originally Team Red had a female member. A badass jaguar shape-shifter called Carilla."

"She meant more to you than that." He'd hidden his thought quickly, but not quickly enough.

He gave a wry grin. "Yeah, okay, we shared a bed once in a while, but we weren't love's young dream. Or even love's old dream. You ever have a fuck buddy?"

Ania thought of the man she'd known in university. Afterward, they'd gone their separate ways, promising to keep in touch. They did, but only a couple of times a year, by email. She supposed that counted. "Yes," she said.

She didn't see any rejection of her in Johann's eyes and felt glad. Too often boyfriends grew too possessive, and although she was fast coming to realize that this was the most intense, most meaningful affair she'd ever had she didn't want to disrespect the half dozen men who'd gone before him. Except for one, who'd turned out to be a bastard, but she reckoned one in six wasn't bad.

"Well, Carilla was like that, until she met Jack. And like your brother said he was an archivist, working at a university library. Instant adoration on both sides. She converted him their first week together. And then she died. Lured into a trap by Bennett and murdered. So any operation against Bennett is personal and I won't rest until we've caught him and neutralized his clinics."

"So Bennett is your nemesis."

Johann grimaced. "We first encountered him when he was running a sleep lab at John McIver University, New York. It turned out to be a cover for the experiments on Talents and a way of contacting them. After talks, the IRDC decided to go along with STORM's request that they cease their illegal experiments and they requested Bennett to stop. Bennett decided not to and he had two of the IRDC's agents assassinated along with two STORM agents—only the STORM agents survived. One of them was Chase Maynord." He nodded when she gasped. "Oh yes, we all have a score to settle with that bastard, one way or another. We since discovered that Bennett had quite an operation, with secret labs the IRDC claims it knew nothing about. Like we believe that. But they do want them closed, so they're supposed to be working with us to make it happen. If they don't, they're the bad guys and we can get the government to close them down, so it's in their interests to get it sorted out. But Bennett has proved elusive so far. We'll get him, hopefully sooner rather than later."

She listened and assimilated. "So Team Red is you, Chase and Jack?"

"And Ricardo Gianetti." He glanced away and she sensed reticence in his mind.

"Gianetti? Haven't I heard that name before?"

"His brother, Sandro, used to be Team Red's leader. He's in Washington now, the first openly Talented senator." Light dawned. Yes, she remembered.

"So what has Ricardo against Bennett?"

"Another victim. Ricardo used to be an artist, poet and painter. Sandro was proud of him and worked hard to keep him away from STORM. He was beginning to enter national competitions with his art, really make a name for himself, but Bennett kidnapped him and used him. We got him out, but Bennett had him for months."

"What did he do to him?"

Johann shook his head. "You don't want to know."

A few images flashed through her before Johann suppressed them. A man, lashed to a table, one arm laid open to reveal the veins and sinews. And he was conscious. The same man, starved, shivering, his head — nobody could survive that.

"He did. But he changed. He joined STORM, and he's ruthless, as if he was born to the life. Sandro told us to look after his baby brother, but Ricardo doesn't need anyone to look after him. Sometimes we need protecting, sometimes we need to do the protecting." He took her hand and caressed her palm, studying the lines on it as if he could read them. Perhaps he could. "So now to what we have planned. We're taking down the club."

"The vampire club?"

"The same." He glanced up. "The day, or rather night, after tomorrow, to give Ricardo a chance to get here from Seattle. I don't want you involved in the operation, but we might need Andros to get us in."

She knew she'd be more hindrance than help, but she still wanted to be there when it went down. But not Andros. "No. He can't. I'll do it."

"He's already volunteered. We need an in, Ania, and they dislike you, they know you're suspicious of them and you resent them."

"Did they bomb the apartment?"

Johann shook his head. "We don't know yet, but they could have. It seems likely. They knew where you lived, and once they realized you were in touch with STORM, they might have decided to silence you. I'm sorry."

Ania swallowed back her tears of self-pity, despising herself for even thinking about her plight. "I've been so stupid. I thought Sheila was a friend, and at first when she took Andros to The Pit I encouraged him. Anything, I thought, that would make him better. She took me for a fool, milked what was left of my accounts and wrecked my reputation. Andros met with nothing but worse health. They used us and I let them."

She lifted her head and stared at the ceiling, long shadows falling across it from the reflections of the table lamps, dimmed to diffuse the light. So she didn't see his sudden movement but she found herself in his arms. Warm and safe. It felt so good, but she couldn't depend on it. Everything she'd depended on so far had fallen apart at the seams.

"Aren't you forgetting something? You were exhausted. Lack of sleep does strange things to a person. You lose your ability to concentrate and you can't think straight when you do. Your mother was ill for a long time. I've seen cancer patients in the last stages of the disease. It's not easy for anyone, least of all the caregivers. When did you give in and let her go to a hospice?"

"Never. I got a night nurse for the last two months." Staring at the ceiling seemed easier right now and it kept her tears at bay. "She wasn't too good, but at least she could cook, so she did that. Besides, I wanted to care for my mother. I didn't want a stranger doing — attending to her personal needs. She was always a proud woman, some would say distant. Andros would. But not me. She encouraged me, loved me and I was glad I could do something for her." She blinked and forced herself to look away, at her new lover, the one her mother would never meet. "I helped her die. I gave her too much morphine. Not all at once, but over the course of a couple of days." She shook her head. "I don't know why I'm telling you that. I'm sorry."

"And that's what's eating you up, isn't it?" Johann wouldn't let her go when she tried a halfhearted attempt at pulling away. "No, I'm not reading you, but it doesn't take a mind-reader to work it out. Listen, Ania. In cases of terminal cancer, that happens more often than not. I've lived a long time, watched friends of mine die. I helped a couple and talked to doctors about it. They told me that it's often the way. Nobody deliberately kills them, they just ease their way a little.

The medication is to stop the pain. And only ever at the request of the patient. Did your mother ask you?"

She nodded, then shook her head. "She wanted it. But she asked me to stop the pain, said she couldn't stand it anymore. She didn't ask me to kill her."

"You didn't." He pressed a soft kiss to her brow. "I promise. Something had already done that for you. You did the right thing."

"You believe that?"

"I do."

Ania felt a weight lift away from her. Whether her guilt had left her or it was merely the result of sharing her anxiety with someone, she didn't know, but hearing it from someone else reassured her, told her she was right. She hadn't told Andros, who'd never been close to their mother and in any case had his own problems. He'd probably be angry if he heard she'd kept that kind of information from him, but now she could face the fact that he would probably agree with Johann.

One night Andros had talked over the possibility of suicide if his Becker's got so bad he couldn't bear it, but in his case he'd need help. The disease would take away all his muscle function. Ania found it hard to promise him she would, but in honesty she didn't know if she could bear to see him suffer as badly as she'd seen in some of the hospices she'd visited. And that had fueled her desire to find a cure or something that would at least halt the progression of the disease. Nobody should suffer like that. Nobody.

And she should hate the man who'd told her that vampires weren't the answer, that neither the donation of blood or the reception of it would provide the cure she and her brother so badly wanted this side of death for the vampire involved. But she didn't hate Johann. She was very much afraid that she loved him.

But she could bear that. She could bear anything, she told herself, and prayed she was right. She'd get through this somehow.

"Hey. Come to bed now. We can't do anything else tonight. Chase is planning the raid on the club, so that will happen soon. And we'll keep a close eye on your brother. Okay?"

She forced a smile. "Okay."

Chapter Eleven

ഇ

Ania would have sworn an oath that she wouldn't sleep that night, but when she felt Johann in her mind, soothing and calming her, she drifted off in his arms, slipping into dreamless slumber almost instantly.

Partway through the night she thought she felt someone slipping into bed next to her and assumed Johann had visited the bathroom, since he felt cold. She heard a male voice. "Hey, baby. All the rooms are occupied on this floor so I guess you won't mind if I share with you. It wouldn't be the first time, would it?" A heavy sigh. "Fuck, the air service gets worse. Next time I'll charter a plane, but at least I know why STORM didn't have any planes available to pick me up. Ready for some action?"

Still half asleep, she fuzzily assumed she was dreaming, so she snuggled against him and felt his arms go around her. And then a chuckle, a masculine one and a comment. "I guess we're not alone then?"

With a squeal, she started awake and realized that Johann lay on her other side, still bed-warm. Johann woke with a shout and shoved her under his body, rolling over her to face the interloper.

"Jesus, Johann, stop that already!" The stranger seemed more irritated than startled. The tussle had pulled the covers off them, and Ania lay stunned by the suddenness of events.

The newcomer was naked. Johann knelt over her on all fours, his teeth bared, his fangs extended and no doubt his eyes shooting fire, although she couldn't see them from where she lay.

As she watched, his muscles relaxed and he sat back on his haunches. Exposing her. She grabbed for the covers but Johann had pushed them aside. So she lay stark naked, exposed to the view of the stranger.

Who didn't hide his reaction to her. As she watched, his cock moved and began to swell. He glanced at it, then at her face. The heat in his eyes warmed her and she felt her nipples tingle and her pussy dampen, as if he were touching them.

"Ania, meet Ricardo. My friend, another member of Team Red, and as you've probably guessed, my fuck buddy."

Silence, fraught and tense, but she couldn't take her eyes off the gorgeous male before her and his reaction was more visible and extravagant. His cock strained, his pupils dilated.

She heard Johann groan. "Damn, Ania, you and Ricardo could burn up the night!"

Hurt lanced through her, destroying the sensuality fast developing in her body. She rolled over and faced him as he straddled her. "I thought that was you and me."

His dark eyes gentle, he put his hand on her waist. "It is, *miláčku*. But sometimes I'd like to show you a little of the wilder side of loving."

"The last thing I want to do is upset you," Ricardo said gently. "I'm sorry. But you are truly gorgeous. Any man into women would get turned-on if they could see you now. Take it as a compliment and be assured I don't want to do anything to hurt you. Ania, my apologies."

A touch of his lips on her bare shoulder mesmerized her. Johann watched her reaction as she shivered at his touch. "You liked that, eh? Don't lie, sweetheart, I can feel it in your mind."

She didn't look away. That would mean she'd have to face Ricardo. And the truth. "How would you feel if I said yes?" She'd be lying if she hadn't admitted it and she had shared a bed with two men before. An experiment in her university years. One she'd thoroughly enjoyed.

His hands spanned her waist, smoothed to just under her breasts. "Relieved. Ania, I want to show you everything you can be, and if you want this, so do I."

"You wouldn't be jealous?"

He smiled. "With any other man, yes. But Ricardo and I have an understanding." He glanced up and she realized he was looking at Ricardo for permission. He must have received it because he turned back to her. He climbed to one side of her, leaving her between the two men. "I told you he was captured and used by the labs a couple of years ago. That's when it happened—when we became lovers."

Another shudder racked her body. What had she gotten herself into? More than that, how could she feel the way she did? Because the thought of two men pleasuring her turned her mind to mush. Sure she'd fantasized, especially in that two weeks they'd been apart, but Johann was so purely male that she hadn't imagined it was possible. Or that he would want it.

Johann spoke quietly, as if he thought she might get scared. "Putting people into rigid groups based on their sexual preferences is a relatively new thing. Post Freud. And both Ricardo and I predate Freud. We've never put our desires in a box."

She'd never thought of it like that before. Used to thinking of people as gay, straight or bi, this was a revelation to her, but she recognized it and accepted it. It made sense, appealed to something hidden deep inside her. Johann continued speaking to her, his voice soft and unalarming. She wouldn't know him as the dangerous vampire she'd seen in the alley a few weeks ago. "Ricardo needed someone who could accept his nightmares and help him through them. He didn't need sympathy or a bunch of head doctors. So I helped, as I know he'd help me."

Three hands on her now. One lay just above her waist, warm and unthreatening. "We also shared women sometimes." Ricardo spoke now, his voice with its slight Italian accent a piquant contrast to Johann's velvet tones, which were wholly American unless he was speaking in his native tongue. "It pleases us both to bring a woman to the heights, to pleasure her together as one man cannot." Johann touched his lips to her forehead. She felt the heat of the other man against her back and knew Ricardo had moved closer. But if she said no, she knew they'd back off and Ricardo would take the sofa.

"Ania, will you let us love you?" Johann said.

Silence fell. What could she say? Then she knew. Felt it with a certainty down to her bones. "May we take it slowly? So that if I say no you can stop?"

Soft lips touched her spine at the top. "*Si, madonna. Bella.*"

Another kiss, just below where he'd planted the first. She raised her head and gazed up at Johann, who rested on one elbow gazing down at her face. She wanted his reassurance. He loosened his hold on her, but only so he could caress her and make space for his partner. Her other lover, if she allowed it. "What Talent does Ricardo have?" His lips trailed a path down her spine, taking his time, making her feel every touch. She thought she knew but she wanted to hear it again.

Johann smiled. "He's a shape-shifter, *miláčku*. A dragon."

She caught her breath. "I've always wanted to see a dragon."

"You will. I promise you that." That faint accent was purely sinful. "Anything you want, we're here to give it to you."

Johann slid down beside her and took her lips in a deep kiss just as Ricardo reached the top of her ass.

He licked it as if he wanted to make a meal of her and she shivered at the faint rasp of his tongue, her skin sensitized by his touch. Johann groaned into the kiss. Then she felt an intrusion into the most intimate part of her — her mind.

A flutter, a touch, until she realized he was waiting for her permission. With Johann supporting her, encouraging her, she allowed it. Ricardo slipped into her mind. Just the outer layer, where he could read her and know if he did something she wouldn't like. The intimacy drove her crazy and for the first time she realized that Johann was there too, but deeper. He'd seeped inside and she'd let him until they existed together. His mind froze when he too realized. *Do you mind? Should I leave you? I know how dearly you hold your privacy.*

She didn't hesitate. *No. Stay.*

The hot breath on her face told her he hadn't been sure of her response and she liked that. He hadn't taken her for granted, hadn't just seized. He could; she knew how weak she was next to Johann. His power awed her sometimes and made her a little afraid. Now here she lay, sandwiched between a vampire and a shape-shifting dragon, and all she could feel was pleasure.

That's how it should be. Just relax and enjoy. Let your responses come naturally and we'll pick them up and act on them.

How sexy was that? To have two men doing what she wanted before she'd even asked? Ania sighed happily.

Ricardo kissed one cheek and cupped the other, his hand large and strong. He massaged and she felt his enjoyment of her shape, the softness of her skin. His fingers spread and he slipped one between her legs. Just held it there, didn't push, didn't insinuate but let her feel it. And his intent.

Johann picked up on her slight apprehension and her growing heat.

Ricardo groaned. "She's getting wetter, Johann."

"Hmm." Johann touched her breast, kneaded it as Ricardo was doing to her bottom. They coordinated their efforts, reading each other through her and for all she knew through each other. She moaned, arching up to Johann, pushing back against Ricardo.

Then Ricardo moved his finger, curved it up to meet the sweet spot between her pussy and her anus. Nobody had ever touched her there before, not so knowingly, and rubbed the skin so carefully, massaging pleasure areas she hadn't known existed before. Her juices made his movements slick and soft, so when he circled her rosebud opening, she only registered an increase in pressure, her nerve endings coming to attention at his touch. Her low moan was involuntary.

Johann slid down the bed so his mouth was at a level with her breasts, but he didn't suck her nipples, not as she wanted him to. His low growl told her he loved the sight as much as did the growing warmth in her mind. "Peaked and hard. Can you make them even harder? They might touch my lips if you can."

The way they felt, they were tying themselves in knots to get to him. But she cheated and pushed her breast toward him. His laugh was muffled when he gave in to temptation and sucked her deep. She felt the tips of his fangs graze her, then withdraw. They were needle-sharp and he was so careful with her.

He lavished attention on each breast, tracing around her nipples with his tongue before sucking them in and curving his tongue lovingly around each one. He sucked and she reached out, gripped his shoulders tightly and felt his warmth suffusing her.

Ricardo slipped the tip of his finger into her anus and wriggled it. Her breath caught in her throat. Forbidden, more than forbidden, but it felt so good.

Relax, don't let anyone else tell you how to live, how to love. This is us, nobody else and what we do is nobody else's business.

Johann was right. It was good.

When she pushed back against Ricardo, urging him to delve deeper, he growled, sounding more animal than human. She loved it. She was learning to accept, not to judge.

"That's right." Johann rimmed her navel with his tongue, delving briefly before going lower. His hands rested on her thighs and as he moved down, he urged them apart. Not that she needed much urging. Ricardo's wicked hands and tongue had taken her up, but when Johann moved down, he moved away, kissing her bottom, finding the sensitive parts of her back. Teasing and arousing. His lips touched her skin, passing on to the next part of unkissed flesh until she was sure he meant to cover it all.

Unlike Johann, who was concentrating on one part of her. He opened her with two fingers, scissoring her wide and rumbling low in his throat when she didn't hide from him, as her initial instincts told her to. "That's it, sweetheart. Open, nothing hidden."

The scent of aroused, hot masculinity rose to her nostrils like the most precious spice, and she wanted, hungered for hot cock deep inside her. Johann caught her thought. "Mmm." He swooped forward and licked her from pussy to clit and then caught her clit in his mouth, nibbling gently before delving deeper with his tongue.

"Oh yes, that feels good." But she didn't say that. Ricardo did. He rubbed his cock against her back, teasing her with the hot, blunt head. "Where do you want this, *cucciola mia*? In your mouth? In your sweet pussy? In your ass? I don't care. I just want you."

Shock jolted her back to awareness. "I-I don't know."

Ricardo crooned next to her ear. "Just let it happen, sweet Ania. Let us love you. We'll know when you don't want something, when you really don't want it. Trust us."

That was the key. She had to let go and trust them not to harm her, two people who could crush her with a thought, turn her mind into mush. And she'd let them in.

Fear touched her but it added spice to her arousal because she'd already made the decision. The rest was up to them. They could take her, use her and she could do nothing. Delicious captivity.

The thought ratcheted her arousal up and below her Johann groaned and slurped. The sound, which should have been embarrassing, stimulated her intensely and she arched her body, pushing herself toward Johann for more.

Ricardo wrenched her head around and took her mouth in a kiss, ravishing her senses just as she reached the peak and came and came, jerking in his arms. His hands curved around to hold her breasts, pinch and squeeze her nipples, and he muffled her cries with his mouth, devouring them as she screamed. His hair, longer than Johann's, fell around her face, curtaining her in dark silk.

Not knowing which way to turn, she twisted and reached out for something, anything. She wanted to hold him. Whichever, whatever.

When Ricardo pulled away, she grabbed for him, but he only laughed, a low, intimate sound that made her rejoice. Because he'd let her into his mind and now she sensed a lingering sorrow that her acceptance of him helped to push back.

He spread his hands, sliding them down her body, encompassing her in his grasp until he reached her buttocks, which he gripped and pulled apart, revealing the cleft between.

Ania wasn't sure she wanted this but before she could protest she felt a finger rimming her anus and she melted. She hadn't known such sensation from that simple touch, hadn't known it was possible. When he slid the tip of his finger inside, she barely registered the forbidden nature of the touch, just that it felt so good. After all, what was one more broken taboo?

The gentle touch firmed a little, became more confident, and fear flashed through her mind. Immediately Ricardo read it and withdrew, but continued to circle the small opening. "Shhh, my beauty. I mean you no harm, no pain." She relaxed again and let him support her, her senses rising again as Johann continued to drink from her.

Ricardo's low, wicked murmur began again. "I can sense you and if you open your mind, you can read mine. It adds to our pleasure, each in the other." She already felt their presences resting in her mind. Now she did as he said, stretched, opened and she found them waiting for her. She couldn't explain how she did it, but it happened. Like three bodies twining together, their minds blended. She saw images, wicked images and her arousal ratcheted up. Some came from Ricardo and some from Johann, and to her shock, some from herself. Images she'd never imagined before.

Johann, still sucking and licking, chuckled and the sound vibrated across her clit before he drew away. Ricardo moved and lifted her, turning her around so she saw shadowy images before Johann leaned over to the nightstand and pressed a button on the remote there. A light came on and he dimmed it to a soft glow.

Ricardo had moved her so she faced a large, full-length mirror set against the wall. There she was, legs spread, thighs glistening with moisture, her breasts cupped in his hands, his thumb and forefinger pulling gently at each nipple. As she watched, his grip firmed and she felt the pressure, adding a pinch of pain to each hard point. She met his gaze in the mirror. Dark, haunted and intense, Ricardo was a man with a past she didn't care to intrude on, even now.

Not so Johann. He came back into view and lay on the bed, opening her pussy lips so they could all see the hard, red clit he'd been tormenting. "So good," he murmured, and leaned up on one elbow, coming closer. "Watch me drink from you, Ania. Watch the way your body responds to me. And feel Ricardo fuck you. Know that I'm watching, feeling, closer than you ever imagined any man."

The hard ridge of Ricardo's cock nudged her back, the dampness seeping from the slit at the top leaving a smear of heat on her spine. He slid lower, widening his knees and lifted her. Johann went with him. The mental connection allowed him to see and anticipate, so awkwardness disappeared. It was almost like a dance.

Ricardo nudged her pussy and she felt fingers—Johann's—opening her for him. Wide open, she still felt the slight resistance as Ricardo slid inside, his thick cock head meeting her hot flesh, inciting sensation every time he moved. Johann moved aside and she saw it in the mirror. His fingers holding her open, his hands cradling Ricardo's balls and that thick, hard cock entering her body, sliding inside, her body enclosing him until he sank it completely within her.

Different. He feels different.

Two male voices blended and harmonized inside her. *You look beautiful.*

You feel so good.

Their accents, faintly Slavic in Johann's case and Italian in Ricardo's, were more pronounced when they spoke telepathically. She never noticed Johann's when he spoke aloud.

It turned her on like nothing before. They must have read the surge of arousal because they continued to murmur to her, telling her how lovely she looked, how desirable until Ricardo tugged her hair, dragging her head back to take her in a deep kiss, penetrating her mouth as deeply as her cunt.

She heated, combusted and without warning Ricardo withdrew and thrust. If he hadn't been holding her steady, his hands on her rib cage just below her breasts, she would have jerked out of reach, so powerfully did his deep fucking affect her. He tore his mouth away and leaned back. Cold air surged between them.

The leverage gave him the purchase he needed to set up a hard, relentless rhythm, and this time he struck her sweet spot.

Johann groaned. "*Miluji tě!*" He sucked her clit into his mouth, letting his tongue play along its length and curl around it, varying the sucks. *You look so good. I want you to come and come for me. Don't stop. Let it all turn into one long climax. Let go, let us care for you, fill you full of us.*

When Ricardo put one finger back on her anus and massaged, she howled and her pussy convulsed.

Ricardo came. She felt his semen, hot and plentiful, jet into her, and then felt Johann lick and taste the mingled juices that seeped out of her. That set her off again, but Ricardo's grip on her tightened. Otherwise she'd have fallen.

Johann straightened up, rising before her, his chest damp with sweat, his lips wet. He thrust his cock between her thighs and as Ricardo withdrew from her, they touched tips. Ania felt the contact as they did and shuddered at the kiss of sensitive skin to sensitive skin. They pushed against each other and lifted a little, bringing them into contact with her. Now she groaned. Her hands went up, grasping, seeking and she found Johann.

Who pushed into her. Ricardo lifted his hands to cup her breasts and Johann glanced down, smiled and then looked back up at her face. "This is what I wanted for you, Ania. This and more. I'm going to make you come and you can discover how different two men can do this to you. We'll have you again and you'll have us. And you will never, ever forget tonight."

She already knew that. A hard cock drove into her, but she didn't need to see the man in front of her to know it was Johann. So different to Ricardo, and to her, better.

Johann spoke against her lips, his eyes caressing her face, and he lifted one hand to brush back a stray lock of hair. The tender gesture spoke volumes, but still not enough. "I won't share you with anyone else but Ricardo. You hear?"

She nodded and he eased her lips open with his tongue, sliding it between them to take her in a kiss of welcome.

Where Ricardo had been hard and needy, Johann grew gentler, softer, and his friend took his cue from him, his grip on her breasts loosening so he could stroke the tender slopes and weigh them in his hands. The movement lifted her nipples against Johann's chest so they rubbed against the hair there, adding to the sensations rippling through her body.

Johann found her G-spot effortlessly but only allowed his cock to touch it briefly with each stroke, increasing her arousal slowly. But if she'd thought that might return some control to her, she would be disappointed. The slow burn was as devastating as Ricardo's violent fucking.

Johann watched her, never taking his gaze from her as he moved in and out of her, and Ricardo urged her to arch forward, pressing his body against her back, making her aware another man knelt behind her, preparing to take her again. Already his cock had begun to rise to the challenge and pressed insistently against her back.

Every time Johann pulled out she heard the sound of her wet flesh resisting his withdrawal before dragging him back in. She tipped her head back and found Ricardo's shoulder. One man supporting her and caressing her while another fucked her. The thought sent her up higher.

All her fantasies coming to life, so much better than that fumbling encounter so long ago. These men knew exactly what they were doing. And they didn't disappoint.

Ricardo dipped his head to kiss her shoulder and move up to lick her throat. She sighed in delight and he nibbled at the pulse point. A low growl made her focus her attention on Johann. Still watching her, he smiled and his mouth opened a little. It revealed two sharp white points.

His fangs. A frisson of fear shivered down her spine, but it combined with the sensations Johann was building inside her, and like two voices singing, it set up a vibration she couldn't resist.

His mind touched hers, soothing with a velvet caress and then she watched the fangs emerge. No longer afraid, she watched this evidence that her lover was so much more, so different. It was as if he hypnotized her, but she knew that wasn't true. He blinked and released her and only then did she realize she'd been under some kind of spell. *I do it without thinking sometimes. I don't want you to feel under any sense of persuasion, other than what we can do to your body. But know that I want you in every way.*

Ricardo stilled and lifted his head and she knew he watched Johann. He leaned back and slid his hands down so they held her waist, supporting her.

Johann kept her attention. *I want you to see me, know me, in all my forms.* His eyes glowed and she knew it wasn't an illusion. They seemed lit from within, fires burning in the dark depths in the pinpricks of lighter color. He lifted his hands and she watched curving talons grow at the ends of his fingers. *Do I scare you?*

She shook her head. "Does your cock change?"

He smiled. *No. This is all. Well?*

You don't scare me, Johann. I gave you myself, you can do what you want with me and if that includes taking my blood, then take it.

He lowered his gaze to watch where he was still pumping in and out of her. *You humble me.*

Will it hurt?

He shook his head. *I'll make sure it doesn't. But if we do this, it will link us deeper and closer. You'll still have barriers you can use against me, but our connection will be stronger than before. We'll be able to contact each other over longer distances. And you'll feel me in you at all times. It's difficult to explain and not every case is exactly the same, but know that this will deepen the connection.*

Is it like that with all the people you feed from? It didn't sound outrageous anymore. She had to believe the evidence of the gleaming fangs, the burning eyes.

Only if I wish it. And I wish for this. Do you?

With a swift jerk of her head, she gave her permission and she felt the heat from his deep sigh of relief gust over her cheeks.

Shall I go?

With a shock she realized Ricardo was still with them.

Only if Ania wishes it.

"No." It seemed right that they have some kind of witness. Strange, but that was what she wanted. Someone to see and record this thing. She felt no fear. This was Johann, even with the changes, it was still him. She suspected that if she'd fallen for a shape-shifter, she'd see him through the change.

Fallen?

Hastily, she shoved the thought away, buried it deep down where nobody could touch it and lifted her gaze to Johann's face.

He hadn't seen, she would have known for sure. Now she had to fight to hide her relief, but when she saw the intensity in his gaze, she forgot everything else. She didn't need telepathy to tell her he was only waiting for her link with him and for her to signal that she was ready.

If she were any more ready she'd explode.

Her body arched to meet him as he leaned forward, her breasts thrust forward, her head thrown back to expose her throat. When his lips came into contact with her skin, the electricity shot through her whole body. Behind her, Ricardo held her, but did no more although she felt his erection hard against her lower back, even when she pushed her body forward. He was ready for her again.

But all she could think of now was Johann and the way he licked and kissed her skin, raising her vein and her need for him. His cock, still embedded deep inside, began to move again, stirring her senses. As if he moved instinctively. Perhaps he did.

She gasped when she felt the twin spikes of sensation that she knew meant he penetrated her vein. The carotid, wasn't it, she thought, a part of her standing away from the incredible sensations coursing through her.

"He'll take a little from your vein, then reseal it. The carotid is an artery. He won't take that." The voice, spoken, as if to avoid impacting on the mental connection she and Johann currently held, came as a shock. "He can pump endorphins in to give you an orgasm, but I'm betting he wants to give you one another way. It's called the vampire's thank you in some quarters."

She couldn't speak, at the moment all she could do was link with his mind. *Has he done this to you?*

"Oh yes. Just enjoy his gift, beautiful lady." Ricardo's hands came up to cover her breasts again, sliding between her and Johann's chest. He stroked, then tweaked, then pinched, adding exquisite pain. She wanted it, she needed it.

The twin pinpricks on her neck came as a sharp counterpoint to the other sensations and then it sharpened, and she felt him begin to suck. Heat bloomed at the point he was taking her, although common sense dictated she should grow colder. Shouldn't she cool as she lost blood? *He's putting compensatory hormones into you. He injects them before he begins to take. Now,* tesorino, *now he will give you the joy.*

He's already — She couldn't finish her sentence. Heat spread from her neck, encompassing her whole body. She couldn't move, couldn't think so it was as well she had a strong male body to lean against.

Johann's cock hammered inside her, jolting her with every stroke. Warmth rapidly escalated into heat, then a burning flame that seared her core, leaving clean white heat in its wake.

She wasn't aware of her cries until Johann's mouth covered hers. He drove his tongue deep into her. At the same time he looped his arm around her waist and dragged her hard against him, driving into her until he shot wet passion deep inside her, triggering a series of fluttering climaxes. Her pussy gripped and released his cock in a series of convulsions, each one milking more out of him.

He shuddered and broke into a sweat, beads springing up all over his body. She slumped against him, still supported by Ricardo behind her, but increasingly unaware of Johann. When Ricardo tried to separate them, she whimpered and held on to him, her hands slipping over his back.

Ricardo laughed and released her, but before they could fall in a boneless heap on the crumpled sheets, he swung them both up.

Dear God, he was carrying them both, entwined as they were. When she glanced up at him, tearing her gaze away from Johann for a brief second, she saw his eyes, pupils elongated, the color filling the whole eyeball, golden, burning, sparks of red flashing.

He'd partially shifted. His arms and legs were still humanoid, but she felt the roughness of scales against her bare skin. What shocked her even more was that it felt totally normal to her.

Chapter Twelve

ຂວ

Ricardo carried them as far as the bathroom, where he dumped them into the huge tub and sent water cascading over them before he joined them, appearing fully human again. She sighed and wriggled in the hot water, steam clouding around them as Johann turned and lifted her but kept her enclosed in his arms.

Ricardo was the first to speak. Leaning against one side of the ivory porcelain tub, he breathed out in one long sigh. "I consider it a privilege to have witnessed that."

Slowly, sense returned to her.

Johann drew her closer and gave her a soft kiss. His sweetness undid her as his violent fucking had not.

She could hardly bear his tenderness because he'd just shown her how different they were, how they could never possibly make anything of this explosive affair between them.

"Honey sweet," he murmured against her lips. "Your juice, your blood, everything, totally addictive." He smoothed his hands down her in a gentle caress and she tried to block her tears as realization struck her again. Real life, something she should never allow herself to forget. Their lives were too different, they even lived too far apart to consider this anything except an affair she'd compare all others to. She already knew they'd come up wanting.

"You're very precious to me," said Johann. He stole a kiss.

She remembered something she should have asked before. She knew shape-shifters could only conceive at certain times of the month, but she had no idea what time of the month it was. "Was the moon up tonight?"

Ricardo caught her concern at once. "The full moon is a couple of weeks away. I'm only fertile during the three days when the moon is at its fullest."

She turned her head. "I'm sorry, I didn't mean to insult you. But my brother — he's not well. He has MD. Muscular — "

"I know what it stands for, Ania," Ricardo said. "And I'm sorry."

"Thank you."

Ricardo cupped water and poured it over her shoulder, then kissed it. "I understand. It's carried through the mother, isn't it?"

She nodded. She'd faced this problem years before and made her decision. "I don't want to bring a child into the world to see him die. Some mothers decide to abort boys, but if I conceived with someone I cared for and I knew, I'm not sure I could do that. So I took the coward's way out and decided not to have children of my own."

Johann's hands stilled on her body. "I never thought of that."

"Does it make a difference?"

"No." Johann's hands moved again, but she knew it did.

Ricardo explained to her. "Johann is fertile, just not very. Vampire fertility is low, so they don't like to use contraception for that reason. It's highly unlikely he'll make you pregnant, and even then there's a high probability that you will give birth to a child who will become a vampire at puberty and then there would be no risk."

She dropped her head, letting the sorrow wash over her. Of course she'd like a child one day, however vigorously she denied it. "I'm on birth control. I guess I'm just used to double checking."

Johann pulled her back down, so she lay between the two men. "But there's a chance."

"I can live with that." Nearly nil. Nothing was certain in this life.

"I'll use condoms."

She felt his revulsion before he suppressed it. "No. Please." Her revulsion rose to meet his. Now that she'd known the delight of feeling him come inside her, his flesh next to hers with nothing between them, the spurt of his seed inside her thirsty body, she didn't want to give it up. And to her shock, she felt an urge to give up her birth control pills. For him. Because vampires had such low fertility every baby was precious to them and she felt Johann's need, instinctive, as much a part of him as his delectable body.

And another reason why she wasn't the woman for him.

Everything she learned told her that. So why did she still yearn for it, long for more of him? Nothing in her experience before had led her to this, no man, no experience, nothing. Fuck, this was bad.

But it didn't feel bad right now, nestled in hot water between two ripped men. Life certainly had its compensations. She reached up to give Johann a soft, sweet kiss and did the same to Ricardo.

Ricardo had used the dimmer to keep the bathroom light from glaring, but it was still brighter than the bedroom and she could study him properly. His shoulders might be a tad broader than Johann's and his longer, dark hair tempted her to thread her fingers through it and feel its softness. His nose was longer, sharper, a blade slashing between his high cheekbones and eyes so dark they were almost black. While Johann had high cheekbones and dark eyes, his were distinctively Slavic and his face leaner than Ricardo's. If she left aesthetics to decide between them, she'd find it hard, but everything in her leaned toward Johann.

"We should light candles," Ricardo murmured. "Give you some romance. But when I look at you, my body takes over and all I can think of is fucking you senseless." She loved his honesty.

"I like the idea of the candles." Johann's deep voice reminded her of their connection, as if she needed any. "We'll do that."

They wouldn't have time to do everything she wanted before the case ended and Johann went home or passed on to a new assignment, somewhere else. Johann glared at her but said nothing. She was glad of that. At least he wasn't pretending.

"Am I weaker because of the blood I gave you?"

Johann's expression softened and he smiled. "I don't need much and I didn't take much. In a way we're weaker than humans, because they only need water, food, warmth and rest. We need blood as well."

"But you're stronger than us."

"Only after sundown. Otherwise, we're just like anyone else. And you know we're not monsters, don't you?" His hands stilled on her.

A faint touch of anxiety colored his feelings, surprising her. She had to reassure her big, bad vampire secret agent. She wouldn't exactly call him ordinary, day or night. "Yes, of course I know you're people, with the same varieties and characters." That surprised her too, how well she understood. A few weeks ago she would have castigated them all as monsters. Now she knew better and shame washed over her when she recalled her blanket condemnation.

Johann reached for the body shampoo, squeezed out a portion and handed it to Ricardo, who did the same. Then they washed her.

Their hands searched out every part of her, smoothing over her skin, washing every inch, and they punctuated their actions with gentle kisses, lips just touching her cleaned skin. They massaged and stroked until she found it hard to distinguish between them. They urged her to stand, then they washed between her legs, using their hands to clean every crease, until the wetness was more than water. She sighed and reached for the nearest cock, which happened to be Ricardo's. His groan soothed her rising need, but only a little. At least she could give a little back. She watched as a bead seeped from the tip and hung there, glistening in invitation. She couldn't resist, but leaned forward and took the pearl into her mouth.

Gripping the skin beneath, she drew on the head and tried an experimental caress. Ricardo's breathed, "Oh yes!" told her she was doing it right. Ricardo's presence in her mind expanded, stroked and he showed her his pleasure in a succession of rippling colors. Now she believed he was an artist.

Had been. The denial sounded more vehement than she deserved. Ricardo cared about the loss of his art.

He tasted good, of salty spice, sharper than Johann.

Behind her, Johann toyed with her pussy, slipping his fingers between her folds. He left her for a moment and then returned, his fingers slicker, and she sensed something extra. Some kind of oil, softening her skin, easing his way so friction was almost eliminated. He slid his fingers around her and around her anus, sending small waves of sensation through her. She wasn't as concerned as when Ricardo did it. She trusted Johann as she didn't yet trust Ricardo, an instinctive, deep-down trust that she didn't have to think about.

She licked and sucked and Johann slid one arm around her waist and jerked her ass hard against him. His fingers penetrated her, his thumb in her ass, two fingers in her pussy, sliding in almost without resistance. He worked her and she squirmed against him. With one cock in her mouth and another between her thighs, she was in ecstasy.

Johann stared down at Ania, her sweetly arched back moving as she worked her mouth on Ricardo. He glanced up, saw Ricardo, his eyes half closed, one hand in her hair, sifting through the golden strands. To see her servicing his friend sent his arousal up to the heights. He loved Ricardo, would always love him, but never wanted to own him, to possess him, to care for him, as he did for Ania.

Every STORM agent had a private channel, for other agents only. If he could, he'd give her access to that, but he couldn't. If it became known she had access to that, Ania could be considered a security breach, and he wouldn't tolerate anyone doubting her.

Apart from a few terse exchanges, he and Ricardo hadn't used that channel tonight. But now he heard Ricardo's voice. *You're in love with her, aren't you?*

I don't know. He always gave Ricardo honesty and that was the truth. *I care for her, I love her as I love you. But I think so.*

So tonight was a test? To see how much you care for her?

No. That was true too. *I wanted to give her something I couldn't do on my own.*

Then we'd better stop this. Although what she's doing is exquisite, I think we should take control.

He touched her mind, ending with a caress because he couldn't help it. *She loves this, but tonight she needs spoiling. She's lost everything today, everything material in her life is gone.*

Ricardo threw his head back and groaned, abruptly cutting off the private contact. Johann felt his arousal soaring, knew he was close and he knew what he wanted to show her. Before it was too late. He flashed an image to Ricardo and felt his friend almost lose it. Fuck, he shouldn't do that.

Another night we'll let her take control. He felt Ricardo's pleasure that he should already be thinking of sharing this lovely woman another time.

He pushed his thumb and fingers deep inside and began to work her with a purpose. He fluttered his fingers against her G-spot and wriggled his thumb, bending it to ease her anus open a little more. So tight. She moaned and pushed back

151

against his hand. Moisture seeped from his cock and he took a second or two to regain control of himself.

He withdrew his fingers as Ricardo put two hands under Ania's chin, gently forcing her to release his cock. She leaned forward, trying to capture it again, but Ricardo put his hands under her arms and brought her up, but not completely upright, to lean her forehead against his shoulder. He murmured to her, his voice low and serving to push Johann's arousal up a little too. "You know what we want to do, don't you, *tesorino*? Are you okay with that?"

A slight nod and a sense of affirmation in his mind. Johann reached for the lube, which he'd put next to the body shampoo a couple of days ago with this in mind. Hopeful she'd still want him. He wanted her every way, wanted to make her completely his and give her everything he was capable of giving. While he wondered at his powerful urges to share this with her, he'd learned to trust his instincts and he was glad of it now.

They'd have to go carefully. If he wasn't mistaken, Ania was a virgin in this area and her skin very delicate.

The thought of his cock buried deep inside her made him burn for her, want her *now*. Going carefully now was the last thing he wanted to do, but for her sake he forced restraint. Applying a generous amount of lube to the area, he slowly eased two fingers inside her, fingers still lubricated from her sweet pussy juice. It seemed to last forever but if he could live on that he thought he could almost do without blood. Except that her blood was so sweet, the best he'd ever tasted and he could feel it coursing through his system, invigorating him, readying him to give it all back to her.

He'd worked her and eased her enough. He glanced up at Ricardo, who met his gaze steadily, with a smile. He couldn't resist. He leaned forward and kissed the beautiful Italian.

The kisses he shared with Ricardo were nothing like the ones he shared with Ania. This was rough, two men sharing their desire for each other and for the woman between them.

Their tongues tangled and Johann forced Ricardo's down, taking him deep and hard before Ricardo fought back and devoured Johann in his turn.

He didn't have to look at her to know how fiercely this evidence of their previous loving turned Ania on. With her arousal he read confusion and uncertainty, but Ricardo was setting him on fire and he couldn't think straight.

Ricardo ate at his mouth and he reciprocated, tasting the man who'd come to mean so much to him. But not, he realized, the shock lancing through him cool and clean, as much as Ania.

How had that happened?

With their bodies pressed close to her, when he felt Ania squirm against him, his attention immediately returned to her. Hot as Ricardo was, she was hotter. He drew the kiss to a close and pulled back, taking a moment to look at her and accept her beauty. She rested on Ricardo's shoulder, watching them, but not passive. Waiting her turn.

As far as he was concerned, it was always her turn.

His fingers still inside her, still working, he knew she was as ready as she'd ever be. And she wanted him to do it, he felt that too.

"Two cocks inside you, *miláčku*, both working you to the kind of ecstasy you won't experience with one. Do you want us to try? We'll be in your mind all the time and we won't hurt you—unless you want us to." He let his eyes take on the glow of the vampire, letting her see. If she showed any fear he'd withdraw.

She showed none.

With one last twist, he pulled his fingers out of her hot little hole and stared down at her. Ready for him, glistening with invitation. Her eyes, so clear and blue, widened as she watched him. A touch of fear edged her thoughts, not enough to worry him, more a frame for the pleasure that lay within, overwhelming it. Still, he carefully committed it to memory.

He wanted only pleasure for her tonight. He dipped his fingers into the water, rinsed them and let her see his intent. She shivered.

He moved behind her and his cock contacted the base of her spine, leaving damp proof of his fierce arousal. Rubbing and stroking, he worked to increase her sensitivity, reaching around to touch her clit, take it between the finger and thumb of his other hand and work it. While Ricardo held her, he took his cock in hand and guided it between her buttocks, easing it down until he slid around and inside the small, puckered hole. Her fear increased, but so did her sensitivity and the way she responded to him. She pushed her bottom back, opening for him and he slid the very tip of his cock in.

He fed it in, reading her carefully, trying not to let the feel of her hot, silky sheath drive him straight into orgasm. He couldn't believe he'd be ready to come so fast, but he had to pause. He glanced at Ricardo, shot him a wry smile. "This is good."

"I know. In case you didn't notice, I backed off a bit, otherwise I'm not going to last either." Ricardo touched his lips to Ania's fair hair in a kiss. "She's dynamite. If you hadn't claimed her, I'd demand a fair trial."

Johann paused, the cold chill of reason striking through the heat of arousal. The thought froze him. Already he didn't like the idea of not having her in his life.

He concentrated on easing inside her beautiful body. The sight of his cock disappearing inside her blew his mind. The last barrier breached, the last invasion. He'd taken her every way he could, destroyed the memory of everyone but him and Ricardo. Not that he planned Ricardo's presence to be in any way permanent.

Tearing his thoughts away, he pushed in a little farther, pulled out and then in again, groaning when he felt her hot, deep fire. Nearly there. He glanced up at Ricardo, tearing his gaze away from the fascinating sight before him and nodded.

He didn't need to do that, but he wanted the eye contact to confirm the eagerness and agreement he felt in his mind.

They stared at each other for what seemed like forever but in reality couldn't have been more than a second or two. Ricardo gave a brief nod and he heard in their private communication channel. *She's yours.*

He already knew that but he didn't mind a little confirmation.

Ricardo eased Ania's legs up, hooking them over his arms and drawing her closer to him. It would open her pussy and make it easier for him to slide inside the reduced size now that Johann was filling her ass. Johann felt for Ania's mind, went deeper. She loved this, loved the attention and the edge of fear had morphed into excitement. He would give her everything she wanted. Now. He already planned a range of toys so he could do this to her every night if she wanted it, fill both holes and give her the fucking she deserved.

He shared the thrill she felt when Ricardo curled her legs around his waist and she reached up to hold on to his shoulders. His cock slid down her slit, breaching her cunt.

They'd shared women before, but somehow it had never felt like this. Never so good, never so perfect. The three of them fit so well.

Ricardo slid inside, completing the connection. Minds, bodies and desire, all linked, all dependant on each other.

Then Johann moved and initiated the rhythm that would take them to unknown places. Because he knew this was a unique experience, that even if they repeated the exercise it would never feel like this again.

Hot and sweet she sucked him in, released him reluctantly and then he felt the hard ridge of Ricardo's cock sliding against his, only a thin layer of flesh between them. *Ania!* "Okay, honey?" The words came out through gritted teeth as he held his orgasm back.

A low moan served as his response, throaty and full. She twisted, but only so she could see him. Her lips were moist from Ricardo's kisses and he realized the only problem with this position was that it made it difficult for him to kiss her. But he managed it because he craved her taste. He crushed his back against hers, pushed his cock deep inside her ass and took her mouth. His hands took her breasts, cupping them underneath while Ricardo held her steady. He already knew she loved her nipples toyed with so he pinched and squeezed them, gave her a nip of pain before flattening his hands and smoothing them. He loved her nipples, loved how hard they got, how they felt in his mouth, in his hands.

Ricardo powered in and out while Johann kept his cock deep inside. The sensation was so good it almost hurt. He fought, held on, but when he released her mouth and saw her staring at him, her heavy-lidded eyes filled with passion, he knew he had to see her like that every day. All the time.

Concentrating hard, he did his best to memorize the way their minds felt, blending with each other, meshing and melding, with separate jags where their needs and desires moved apart. The differences were as good as the blending, each adding to the unique experience that was this night, this time.

Ricardo's cock rubbed against the underneath of his with every stroke, getting into his stride now. He leaned back a little, using the edge of the half sunken bath to steady his upper thighs, and widened his stance. Ania had her legs curled around Ricardo's waist, and Johann stood up to his lower thighs in water, rock steady while Ricardo did exquisite things to them both.

"Jesus, Ricardo, this never felt so good before!"

Ricardo chuckled, but the laugh quavered as he powered in again, thrusting deep. He lifted Ania a little and Johann realized he'd pushed his lower body against her slit, mashing her clit against him so he could stimulate that too. He grinned, his teeth clenched against coming too soon. Ania wasn't there yet. Little flutters, quivers that shook her told him she was close.

He moved again, working her breasts, now a breath away from Ricardo's chest, and drove his cock back in, his balls meeting her body with every stroke. He didn't have to work to time his strokes—Ricardo thrust in counterpoint, in when he was out, out when he forced it back in.

They changed the rhythm without warning, both hard inside her body, this fierce fucking becoming a dance they never wanted to end, but Ania was building to an explosion and she took them with her.

When she convulsed, her ass squeezed his cock so hard he couldn't hold back once she'd released in the first of several compressions that forced his essence up his cock and into her body. And it felt like his essence, the very heart of him, everything he was leaving him and filling her. He felt its hot passage, pushing its way out as if as thick as mercury. Then he lost it.

Ricardo growled, then cried out. He cried Ania's name, then Johann's. Ania couldn't articulate more than an animal howl.

Claws extended from Ricardo's fingers and his scaly dragon tail curled around them all to circle them in passion. He didn't know if Ania noticed but the sight awed Johann. Shape-shifters sometimes shifted involuntarily, but only when completely out of control and that rarely happened. It was happening now. For the second time that night Johann saw Ricardo's dragon eyes, golden, shot through with sparks of fiery red but he didn't sense the conscious decision to shift.

That meant Ricardo was doing it because he'd released everything, becoming his elemental self, the dragon and the man sharing the same consciousness, the same body. With his own release roaring through him he watched the beautiful creature that Ricardo had become lean back, effortlessly holding them all together with his strong tail. He reached up, covered Johann's hands with his and then squeezed, sliding up to tweak Ania's breasts with his claws. So gently she could only have felt an exquisite stroke. She had her eyes closed, but when she opened them, Ricardo had returned to his human form, except for his eyes, which returned to normal more slowly.

Johann exchanged a smile with him before Ania opened her eyes and gazed dreamily up at Ricardo. Jealousy shot through Johann, but he forced it back. Ricardo had made it quite clear that this was Johann's play, his call, and he had no reason for it. But it seemed he didn't need a reason.

Without a word, Ricardo swung her up into his arms and stepped out of the tub to carry her to the shower. This suite boasted a large walk-in shower, so Johann followed them and touched the buttons that would send the hot water cascading over them.

Ricardo put Ania gently on her feet before he reached for the bottle of body shampoo. He squeezed a puddle out and passed the bottle to Johann. Their hands touched and lingered, both men enjoying the contact, but they turned back to Ania. He loved washing her, feeling her soft skin under his.

Johann felt strangely hesitant, as if giving her the choice between them. She didn't have to do that but now that he'd invited another man into their relationship he felt an uncharacteristic internal doubt. He rarely agonized over decisions. But now he wanted her to choose of her own free will without any persuasion from either side. Ricardo knew, he could tell from the way he too held back, only touching Ania as an assistant would, ministering to her without lingering unduly.

He felt Ania's exhaustion, but he knew she'd recover soon and maybe consent to another round. Because he also felt her total satisfaction. Between them, he and Ricardo had loved her to satiety and given her experiences she couldn't have with just one man.

And that was what he wanted.

Wasn't it?

Chapter Thirteen

ℰ

Strange how the unthought and unusual could become almost normal. When Ania woke up sandwiched between two buff male bodies, she gave each a kiss and climbed over Johann to get to the kitchen area. She needed her coffee. She had to walk a little awkwardly, but they'd cared for her so well she was fine. Or would be in an hour or two.

Finding a robe, she belted it around her and watched as the two men rolled together in the bed, their legs and arms wrapping around each other. But still asleep. They looked beautiful together. She wondered how she'd managed to get into this situation, but she wouldn't get any answers by watching them. She needed that coffee.

Johann had a fancy cappuccino and espresso maker, but it had a filter jug on one side so she ignored all the tubes and steam valves and found some coffee bags. Kenya worked fine for her, so she put that one in from the choice offered on the complimentary tray.

While the coffee bubbled she tried to put things straight in her mind and found herself completely at a loss. Did she have one lover or two? Ricardo was gentle, loving and ripped, but he wasn't Johann. Now that she'd had the opportunity to compare him with someone else, she knew for sure that she loved him, wanted him, but she couldn't have him. Vampire, mortal, New York, LA, nothing worked except the way she felt about him.

They'd both be gone soon. She just had to make the most of what she had.

She sighed, glancing at the laptop resting on the table in the sitting area of the suite. She didn't have one anymore.

She'd better contact her insurance company today, if her minders said it was all right to call them, and arrange compensation for the fire. At least she had some things left, the items she'd put into storage. But she'd lost a lot. Tears filled her eyes when she remembered the precious family photographs she'd never get back, the souvenirs of her growing up, the school books, the prom dress that she'd only ever worn once, the stuffed toys she'd loved as a child.

Perhaps it was time she put all that behind her, but she didn't want to. Especially this way. Today they could find out who did it, who tried to murder Andros and her. She'd been so exhausted she hadn't even bothered to do more than make sure her brother was safe. Already she trusted these people with her life and with his.

But Andros would never find the cure he yearned for. Time and again she'd tried to tell him he should live with what he had, but it was easy for her. She might be a carrier but she didn't have MD, would never have it. Being a carrier was enough. More than enough. It meant she'd denied myself the possibility of children. She couldn't give a child the curse her brother bore. She could have a test, but she didn't trust them, and anyway it was easier to just deny the possibility. Or it had been, before Johann erupted into her life.

The slight risk of pregnancy she'd taken with Johann bothered her, but feeling him inside her body, skin to skin, was too addictive for her to give up. She'd always insisted on a belt and suspenders approach, the contraceptive she took every day and a condom, but she couldn't do that with Johann. She loved it, loved the feeling, loved knowing nothing lay between them when they fucked. When they made love, because they did both.

The coffeemaker gurgled its completion and she opened cupboards to find mugs or cups. Good white china mugs, with the T of the Timothy group emblazoned on each.

She almost dropped one when she felt a soft kiss on her head. How on earth had he crept up on her so quickly? And which "he"?

Ricardo. She found it easy to touch his mind, easier each time she tried it. "Your mental barriers are softening. You'll be doing it instinctively in no time," he murmured. He moved away from her toward the fridge, and opened it to find the cream.

She stared at him. Dark, thick hair touching his collar, or it would have done if he'd been wearing a shirt. As it was, he wore nothing. Stark naked and completely comfortable in that state as she was not, he cocked his head and smiled at her, cream pot in hand. "What?"

She swallowed. "Where do I start?"

He laughed. "Don't worry. I'll be gone soon enough. You and Johann belong together. I'm just a third, a playmate. Nothing more."

"A bit more than that." He'd opened enough for her to read his pain. He'd suffered and although his body showed no scars, his torture had marked his mind. "And he did that to you? The person who destroyed my home?"

His habitual half smile faded and he took the step separating them, tilting the cream pot toward her to ask her if she wanted any. She nodded. "It seems likely. We'll get him."

"What will you do when you find him?"

He glanced at her. "Kill him and close down all the labs he's set up. Only there are more than we thought. He's been planning this for years."

"Planning what?"

"He had an underground network of labs that we're fairly sure the IRDC didn't know about. They tried to pretend they'd been watching him, but they hadn't. Complete bullshit."

"So where are these labs?"

"Worldwide." He leaned against the counter and took a sip of his coffee, completely at his ease. Surprisingly, so was she. "We need to track down a record of them all, then we can close them down. So far we've followed him around the States and closed down the labs as we found them. But he's always been a step ahead of us." He sipped again. "This time we found you. Or rather, Johann did."

They watched each other. If she hadn't found Johann first, would he now be her partner? No, she decided, he wouldn't. Sexy as he was, he couldn't compare to the connection she'd found with the vampire.

In her mind she felt Johann leave the bedroom and turned to capture his first smile of the day.

He never smiled that much before.

I never had much reason to smile. Johann kept her gaze. *Not like now.*

She shivered. That deep connection between them had grown effortless. Even after last night, even with her body tender from their attention she wanted him.

Johann crossed the room toward them, his intent clear in his eyes.

Then the phone rang.

The day went faster after that. No chance to start the day in the best way. They'd slept in, which considering what they'd been doing until the early hours wasn't a great surprise. But it meant they had to start moving, thinking. And she still hadn't seen Andros.

When a knock fell on the outer door, she answered it without hesitation, knowing the guards outside wouldn't allow anyone she didn't know access to her. Compensation for never being alone.

She didn't wait for Andros to enter, but grabbed him and hugged him before dragging him into the room and shoving him down on to one of the big squashy sofas in the living area. "How are you?"

"Fine." Andros shrugged her off and glanced around the room. His gaze stilled when he saw Ricardo.

She was glad the maid had been in to change the sheets and towels, even if Andros might not see them, and she prayed he assumed there were two bedrooms in this suite. But when shame swept over her Johann crossed the room to put his arm around her shoulders. "None of that." *Don't judge yourself by other people's standards.*

He was right and as her mind drifted back over the incredible events of last night the shame left her, replaced by warm anticipation of the night to come, and she wondered what she was turning into.

Someone I want to see fulfilled and happy. Johann guided her to the sofa set at right angles to their own and introduced Andros to Ricardo, who was already sitting there.

Chase came in after a brief knock. He was dressed for business in a charcoal gray suit and crisp white shirt and he carried a folder and a laptop, which he set up on the coffee table in front of them. He sat next to Andros, not attempting to hide the screen from him.

Andros stared at the screen and blinked. With a sharp jerk of his head, he glared at her. "So what is this? STORM? I've been told about them, seen them on the news."

"You've not been paying proper attention though," Chase drawled, every inch the superior businessman. "I'm a member of STORM and I'm a Sorcerer. Ricardo here is a shape-shifter and Johann, as you know, is a vampire."

Andros's eyes widened. "Fucking hell."

Chase hit a button on the laptop. "You've been talking to your vampire friends, haven't you? All the rooms on this floor contain high security alerts, so when you opened your new cell phone, the monitoring went into action. Well thanks for that, it gave us a few new leads."

"You don't have the right!" Andros spluttered. His hand went to the pocket of his jeans where he kept his cell. They must have given him a new one, which meant he knew the number by heart.

Chase shrugged. "So sue us." He glanced around at the others. "When my friends are threatened, all bets are off. I've compared a few numbers, had a few checks done and The Pit is one of the places Bennett uses to harvest his subjects. He's after vamps, but he hasn't had too many from there recently. It seems that most of the members are vampire wannabes."

Johann snorted. "I can't figure why anyone would do that."

Chase gave him a droll look, his eyes a startling clear sapphire-blue. "You can't? Try living forever, super strength and all that glamour novelists have been peddling since Stoker came up with the magic formula."

This time Johann's response was a growl. "Fucking bastard gave us nothing but headaches."

Chase waved his comment aside. "Another wannabe. He got what he deserved. Anyway, the members of this club are alive and kicking, unlike Stoker. It was started three years ago by three vampires."

"Before Talents came out," Ricardo said. Andros, still staring at Johann with a fascination Ania didn't like at all, switched his attention to Ricardo.

"Yes. Quite a few vamps did that as a way of getting food without too much hassle."

Johann grunted. "Not something I've ever approved of."

Chase raised a brow. "And you're the arbiter of all things vampire?" He turned back to the screen without waiting for a response. Ballsy to taunt a vampire, even in the daytime, Ania thought, but when she glanced at Johann, she saw his wry grin.

Chase passed on to other matters. "Okay, so The Pit was doing something not illegal, but that some vampires didn't like. But about two years ago, with an influx of new members, all claiming they were human, things changed. Vampires started to disappear but because this club claimed exclusivity and didn't exactly advertise itself, nobody made the connection that they all belonged here. The victims were chosen carefully too. They had other connections, so the police were sent off on wild goose chases if they got too close." He glanced up and breathed in deeply before returning to the screen. "One of those new members was the woman we have cause to know, Jeanine Parker. Maybe killing her wasn't the best solution because it's alerted them. They've upped security. Another was or is Sheila Murtagh. She had much closer connections than you thought. The owner of the club has been her lover for at least two years and he's a vampire."

Ania felt the full weight of the heavy silence that fell then. If she'd felt stupid before, it was nothing compared to now. She really knew nothing about Sheila after all. Tears filled her eyes and before she could blink them away, they spilled over and fell.

With a protesting cry of "No!" Johann dragged her into his arms and despite her best efforts to pull away, kept her there. At least she could dry her eyes on his soft t-shirt. Another hand touched her shoulder. Ricardo. Two protectors. Just what she needed if anyone was to take her seriously. Not.

"It wasn't her fault," Johann protested fiercely.

"Nobody says it was," Chase said mildly. "Murtagh targeted her. The business got her into the places she needed, not least the Timothy. For what it's worth, she took me too. I didn't have much to do with her, but I trusted her and I didn't read her like I should have done."

Ania struggled to get free and Johann released her a little, but only so she could sit up. He kept his arm around her shoulders and pulled her close. Ricardo moved close and kept his hand on her thigh.

Andros stared at the hand, then up at her face. She struggled not to blush. She had nothing to be ashamed of, even though she suspected that everyone in this room knew what had happened last night.

She couldn't bear it. She'd never done anything like this before, and yet she had enjoyed herself so much she couldn't deny she wanted to do it again.

Good, because I want it too. Hold your head high, it's not like we're parading through the streets naked.

A flash of heat seared the room and Ania blinked, startled. She knew Johann's mental signature, was getting to know Ricardo's, and it hadn't come from either of them.

Chase. Was that his thing? Chase avoided meeting her eyes and cleared his throat.

Aha.

That made her feel a little better, although she still had Andros to confront. If he dared mention it to her.

"So. The Pit," Chase reminded them. "Sheila's a member of the IRDC, had been for years, or so they tell me. I got the email confirming it about half an hour ago. At some point she hooked up with Bennett and she got herself into The Pit to get victims for Bennett's experiments. She put enough money into Simply Service to keep you going, not enough to make you wonder where it was coming from. After Talents came out into the open, she began to milk you. She'd thrown her lot in with Bennett and she used the contacts from the company to feed the club." Chase's mouth flattened with distaste. "She was building her own empire. Until we fucked things up for her."

He leaned back, stretching his arms above his head. When he relaxed, his suit jacket settled around him in a perfect configuration that spoke of the made to measure. Effortless class, the kind Ania had tried for all her life and failed to achieve. Budget clothes and a sense of style could only go so far.

"You were getting too close to them, Ania. You'd been doing online researches. Chances are they had your laptop bugged, implanted a virus so they could keep track of what you were doing. So you did something that threatened them, though I'm not sure what it was." He sighed. "It's all academic now. All burned to ashes. Not that it matters much, they know you're on to them."

"I don't know either. But I kept everything on my laptop, all the financial records, the company records and personal data too, so they could have wanted anything."

"We have to take care of you, guard you day and night."

She stared. "And I get no say in that?"

Chase's cool blue eyes bored into her. "Well if you want, you can say goodbye to all of us and cope on your own. But Johann might object to that because they'd most likely kill you. They weren't exactly going for survivors the other day." Sarcasm etched his voice in acid. "My guess is they didn't realize Johann was in there with you, either that or sunset took them unaware." He glanced at Johann. "Only vampires are hyper-aware of when the sun goes down."

She swallowed. Against the IRDC or this Bennett character, she had no chance. "You know I can't do that."

Chase's tone softened. "We could send you away. Somewhere Bennett can't find you. Witness protection, if you will."

"And Andros?"

"Him too."

The thought tempted her. But a few things militated against it. "Andros has exams in the next few weeks. Important ones."

"Shit." Johann glanced at Andros, still sitting silently next to him. But his seeming docility didn't fool his sister for a minute. "You'll do those exams with a bodyguard, kid."

Andros opened his mouth at last. "I'll do whatever I see fit to do. If I want to go to Bennett and tell him everything, I will." He lifted his hands, ran them through his hair in a gesture Ania knew well. He wasn't just worried, he was tired. Running on empty. "But I won't. All I wanted was a chance to cure my MD. The guys at The Pit said they could do it. But you told me they can't."

Johann shook his head. "I'd like to kill the fuckers for that. Andros. If a vampire converts you, he dies. So from the vampires you know, do you think that's possible? Any martyrs you know about?"

Andros stared at Johann who met his gaze solidly. He broke the contact and glanced at Chase, who nodded. "Don't look at me, I have the same lifespan you do. And the same vulnerabilities."

Andros' fist came down on the upholstered sofa arm. "Fuck!" He growled, low in his throat. "They took me for a complete and utter fucking idiot, didn't they?"

He bent forward, his head between his hands, the picture of despair.

Chase's voice remained steady and reasonable. "No, they just kept you sweet. You're food to them, that's all. And if Bennett's people were involved, their insurance policy. You'd be a hostage to Ania's good behavior. I get the feeling the IRDC is more involved than their spokespeople admit, but I could be wrong."

Ricardo grunted. "It's been known."

Chase threw a glance his way. "More than once." He opened his eyes wide, wider, before leaning back in his chair and staring at the ceiling. "Look, guys, I'm running on empty here. I haven't seen Jillian for almost twenty-four hours. She's holed up in our suite and she's going stir crazy. So I'll cut it short. We're putting agents in another hotel to pose as Ania and Andros. They'll be well guarded, but the trail will lead to them, not here. We'll raid the club as soon as we can, most likely in a couple of days, once we've scoped the place out and planned it as far as we can. Simplest is often best. Any questions?"

"Nothing. Except I want Ania guarded closer than close."

Chase met Johann's gaze. "That, my friend, goes without saying."

"And how do I feel about it?" Ania demanded.

Chase grinned. "I'll introduce you to Jillian. You can complain together, work out a fine revenge if you want. But at least you'll be alive, if mad as hell. It'd be stupid to say we take care of our women and keep them out of the way, I know that, but it'd be equally stupid to ignore the danger."

She hated it, but she had to agree. "I guess. But surely there's something I can do?"

"Yeah." Chase passed his hand over his eyes again. "I'm going to fall over soon if I don't get some rest. I know you're pretty competent with computers. So if I leave this laptop with you, can you get up to speed and do some more research? I want a plan of The Pit, blueprint if possible. That's a long shot, but if you can use one of those street photo sites we might get to know where the exits are."

Andros said, "I'll sketch it out for you."

Chase gave him a nod of thanks. "I'd appreciate that. I'd like more precise measurements, but maybe that's asking too much. The second task is that I'm trying to locate the Bennett labs. When we raid that club, they'll know we're on to them and they might try to clear out, so if we can locate it, we raid that too. All the information we have is on the laptop, but the club has priority. That laptop is not to be hooked up to the Internet, I'll send you another for that, because it has all the information we have collated on it. We don't want to risk any leaks now. Do you think you can handle that?"

"Sure." Relieved she'd have something to do, Ania accepted the task with alacrity, but frowned at Chase.

"I'll put other people on it too, but you have insights, local knowledge that we could really use right now."

Stillness fell while they waited for her to answer. She didn't keep them waiting long. With a sharp nod, she assented. It made sense. She could be a liability if she tried to tag along with them to the club. So could Andros.

"You need my brother to get into the club."

Chase sighed. "It's the easiest way."

Andros shrugged. "I don't care. They've screwed me over so the least I can do is return the favor."

"He'll get us in, then I'll send him out with someone before we close the place down," Ricardo told her. "If I have to bring him back myself, I will."

"I'll do it," Johann said suddenly. "I'll flash him right back here. Quicker that way."

She shot him a grateful look. Used to caring for her brother, she didn't like the idea of handing over his welfare to others. Even to himself. But if she couldn't be there, the next best thing would be Johann, who wouldn't risk Andros because he knew how much her brother meant to her.

Chase got to his feet. "I need rest and I need to see my wife," he said, so frankly that Ania could only admire his candor and wish for it for herself. "We know what we're doing now. Andros will get Ricardo and Johann into the club and we'll station agents around the exits and wait for the signal."

"So we're to find out what we can before the raid?"

Chase rubbed the back of his neck. "That's about it. I'm a big believer in the KISS rule. Keep it simple, stupid."

He left to the sound of laughter, which hushed almost as soon as he'd gone.

Tension descended. Ania felt it in every pore of her body. Ricardo's hand tightened on her thigh and Johann's arm around her shoulders went rigid. But neither man withdrew.

Andros stared at them, taking his time, his gaze sweeping up and down her, excoriating her with his glare. "Tell me it's not true." In contrast to his eyes, his voice remained calm and quiet.

"What? You know Johann and I—"

"And this guy?" Andros jerked his head in Ricardo's direction. "A Talent whore now, are you?"

Johann was on his feet, standing in front of Ania. She saw the way he shook as he raised his hands.

"Johann!" Ricardo's sharp bark brought his hands back down to his sides and his shoulders rose as he took a couple of deep breaths.

"If anyone else but you had said that, you'd be dead by now. You have no right to condemn her —"

"He has every right," said Ricardo, his Italian accent more prominent than usual. "He's her family. Her brother. But not to call her names in front of others. That is not an honorable way to proceed."

Ania craned her head to one side to see her brother's face. As she'd expected, he'd set his jaw, determined to face these terrifying monsters. She didn't know if he'd seen a vampire in full vampire mode, but she guessed he might have done. And what he faced now wasn't a mere man. Johann was a trained agent with all that implied. He could probably kill with his bare hands at any time of the day or night.

The man still sitting next to her could transform and kill Andros, but when she opened her mind, as they'd taught her, most of the aggression came from Johann. But Ricardo was angry, no doubt about that.

"You should not judge what you don't understand," he said now. "Whatever Ania does is her choice. I would prefer that you not call her those names, though."

Andros's sneer wasn't his best look. "If she sleeps with every Talent that comes her way, what else is she?"

She tried to become the voice of reason. "I haven't slept with Chase. Or any of your vampire friends. Andros, this is my business. If you don't want to know, don't ask, but Johann has showed me the greatest joy I've ever felt. He knew I wanted this."

Ricardo gave her leg a brief squeeze. She swallowed. It had made her feel sick to confess it to her brother, but it was the truth and she should honor it. Last night, she hadn't been a passive participant. She'd wanted it and she'd loved it.

She wanted it again. But she also wanted Johann to herself sometimes. While she didn't understand where these feelings came from, she had enough honesty to admit it, at least to herself. And the two guys, she realized a little belatedly, because Johann was flooding her with warmth, his anger abating to a controllable level. He stepped aside, allowing her a clear view of her brother.

He stared at her now, puzzlement coloring his eyes. "I don't think I understand you at all sometimes."

"I don't know myself some days." She tried a grin. He didn't return it, but his expression softened a little.

"Just don't flaunt it, okay?"

As Ricardo began to get to his feet, she gave him that concession. "Okay, okay. You have to live in this town, right?"

"Yeah." Andros shoved his hands in his pockets. "Something like that."

"And we all know how moral students are," Johann added.

Ricardo cocked a brow. "In my day, they were."

Johann shot him a glance. "Don't blow his mind completely."

Andros' gaze went from Johann to Ricardo and back. "Who's the eldest?"

Ricardo raised a brow. "I'm never quite sure. Johann's as coy as a girl about his age."

"Maybe I don't want to blow *your* mind."

She blew out a breath. "Fuck, guys, the testosterone is getting so thick I won't be able to find my way to the door soon. Lay off it, will you?"

Johann glanced at her and she felt him deep in her mind. Only he knew how rattled this made her. Three men, where she hadn't managed even one before, and two of them her lovers. She was still reeling from that, couldn't imagine how or why she'd done it, but it felt so right at the time.

Chapter Fourteen

ಐ

"You guys ready?"

Johann glanced at Chase and fought past the thick aura he'd spread around himself to fuzz his identity. Nobody looking at the tousle-haired, surly man dressed in well-worn jeans and an even more worn t-shirt would have recognized the urbane hotel owner, but just in case, Chase used his considerable psi ability to surround himself with a strong persuasive "don't look at me" glamour.

Johann had something similar, in case anyone recognized him, but his was more cursory. He'd dressed in black and wore a studded leather wrist strap and collar to enhance the Goth look but the people standing in line outside The Pit easily outclassed him. He stared, enjoying the sight of so many pale-faced, black or red-haired people dressed in mixtures of black, white, silver, red and the occasional flash of plaid. One smiled and he saw a flash of fang. Not like his long, thin, razor-sharp fangs, the ones he kept hidden most of the time, but an eye-tooth filed to a point, or maybe a fake cap. He hoped for the latter. Filing could ruin the teeth.

He felt slightly queasy now. He lifted his hand to run it through his hair, a habit he'd never quite broken, and then shuddered at the feel of the heavily gelled spikes Ania had helped him achieve before he left. First thing he'd do when he got back was to get under the hottest shower he could bear. Hopefully not alone.

Some of the people in the line wore pendants around their necks, bearing, he knew, blood from their loved ones or maybe even their enemies. The risk to health didn't bear thinking about. Not his, he was immune, but theirs. In fact he could

175

catch illnesses, but as long as they didn't kill him in twelve hours he was safe because the vampire part of him defeated them. He'd had AIDS more than once but he didn't have it now.

He wouldn't feed here tonight unless he had to. Unless he was wounded or needed an extra boost and the way they'd planned the raid, that wouldn't be necessary. But sometimes plans didn't work out.

They had someone watching every exit, each one manned by at least one bouncer and Jack monitored all of them, linking them by computer and by telepathy. He was stationed in a discreet surveillance vehicle a block away. When the time came they'd jettison discretion.

Chase was directing from the front. Team leader for this gig, although Johann had done his share of leading missions. Chase knew LA better than he did and had contacts, although East Coast and West Coast moneyed classes were extremely different, threads were maintained through the elaborate network of family and influence, shared investments and interests. And it gave Johann the freedom to do what needed doing, to take the initiative if his specialist knowledge—vampires—gave him cause to do so.

He enjoyed the adrenaline coursing through his system, the heightened awareness and the sense of danger it brought, but new to him was the edge of concern and worry for Ania. And what all this would mean to her.

Andros glanced around and nodded. He and Chase were substituting for the musicians who usually formed Andros' band. Time to go. Carrying the instrument cases and amplifiers they had no intention of using, they stepped forward.

Johann felt Andros' tension increase. He'd locked in to him deep, determined not to let him go for a minute. He was important to Ania, therefore he was important to him too. Monitoring for a spike in his fear, when he might give himself away, Johann stepped up close behind him, keeping in his shadow. The single light over the entrance glared down on them. Not even a stage entrance? Yes, there it was. Andros had paused to say hello to the muscle on the door, who even managed to crack a smile. He'd bet. Johann scanned the man. So there was at least one genuine vampire here tonight.

They followed Andros around the corner of the building into an alley where he had to be careful where he put his feet, toward another door with a dimmer bulb set into its shallow canopy. More muscle, but this time no smiles. The man glanced at Andros, put his finger to his ear and let them in. Since the muscle on the main door had probably contacted the one here telepathically, the finger on the ear was a bit of dramatic overkill, but Johann could live with that.

Dragging the amp and guitar case through the narrow door proved a challenge but at last he got through, only to face Chase's grin and Andros' exasperation. He shrugged. "What?"

Andros huffed and turned away, his sneakers squeaking on the chipped, scratched vinyl floor, a dull shade of red that Johann imagined would once have been a lot brighter. His own feet stuck to the floor with every step, beer rather than blood, he guessed, but he lifted the equipment and followed the guys down a long hallway, then another, narrower one. A dull thump reverberated through the floor, increasing as they approached the door that led to the stage. When they opened the door the recorded music swelled and broke over them, a heavy, rhythmic thud overlaid by a screeching guitar. Over all that, a hoarse scream indicated vocals. Johann liked rock, but his taste leaned toward something with a tune to it. This place made him feel old-fashioned, but he'd grown used to that over the years.

The stage proved to be a small platform raised about eighteen inches above the dance floor. Already the place heaved with bodies, all in Goth mode. Customers decorated the long, padded seats that lined the large room and also sprawled over the benches and stools scattered over the seating area. The dance floor still provided room and people stood three deep in the area before the bar.

Masked lights illuminated the club, including wall panels decorated with masks and images, all of vampire symbols, but only the symbols available to the general public. Johann didn't see any sigils, the family signs that identified a vampire, seared into his mind at birth. He'd concealed his own behind a heavy mental shield. Only a Sorcerer as powerful as Chase could breach it now.

He glanced at his colleague. Chase had opted to gel his hair slick with his head, making his fine-boned features almost skull-like, only emphasized by his lack of tan. He fitted well into this place.

A few people lifted a hand in greeting and Andros returned them. They went through the farce of setting up the equipment. A drum kit already stood in its place and they propped the cheap, disposable guitars next to it. They weren't due to deliver the set for another half-hour, which was just as well because Johann just about knew one end of a guitar from the other but had no idea how to play it.

He jumped down from the stage and forced his way through the throng to the bar. He couldn't drink after sundown without severe consequences, but he wanted to pretend, as part of his cover. Anyway, it meant he could mix and maybe hear something.

One raised area to the left of the bar was roped-off and people sprawled on what looked like leather seats, their drinks on glass coffee tables. A cut above the hoi-polloi like him. One man sat in state there, surrounded by acolytes. A bit like a vampire king and his court. Johann stopped his snigger, but his lip curled.

The man turned his head and snagged Johann with his gaze. Dark, glittering, handsome. The guy certainly had his share of good looks. Johann lost the sneer, tried to look cowed but it was too late. The man lifted a finger and beckoned to him. Glancing around, Johann saw the muscle approaching him. Seemed he had no choice. Some fucking vampires didn't deserve the honor.

An attendant standing by the ropes unhooked one side for him and hooked it again after he'd passed through. Philosophically, Johann crossed the carpeted area—black, of course—and stood before the bastard, who got to his feet.

Johann topped six feet comfortably but this vampire had at least three inches on him, which would make him around six-five. That figured. He'd always found kowtowing unpleasant, but he'd do his best, ease this guy along until he found out more of what they needed to know. Any link with Bennett, a hint as to where the labs were, maybe the location of Bennett himself.

So he spread his senses a little and found the man open. He read his family without too much surprise. They were always arrogant fuckers, the Hunters.

Chase lurked at the back of his mind, ready to transmit anything he found to Jack outside. *All in position,* he assured Johann on their deep link. *Ready to go when we give the word. I'm mingling at the other side of the club. Let's see what we can find out before I give the word.*

Go for it.

The man looming before him stared at Johann, frankly assessing him. Johann put up with his stare but felt exasperation rise within him. Wryly, he admitted that the problem might be partly his, because humility had no part in his nature.

While he waited for the demon king to speak, he studied the people who formed his court. Yes, court didn't seem inappropriate in this context, although he'd met more impressive entourages in his time, hell, he'd even had them himself. The man clanked when he moved. A waistcoat festooned with chains worn open over his bare chest. Bare except for a pair of nipple clamps and a chain linking the two, that was. Johann guessed this guy wasn't into sub behavior. More likely he wore the chains to show how tough he was.

Great. Bravado had never appealed to him unless it was absolutely necessary.

He felt a buzz as Hunter tried to read him. He allowed him into the outer level, which he'd primed with his mortal alter ego, the cover he wore when he didn't want to be recognized as a vampire. Quickly, he spread his senses. Six Talents in this pseudo-VIP area. The rest were mortals or deeply shielded.

The vampire standing before him looked his fill. Johann presumed he was supposed to be intimidated, but instead he pasted a bland expression on his face and scanned the area, widening with each circuit until he touched a familiar aura— Chase. They had the area covered between them.

"Where are the usual members of the band?" His voice came out in a low rumble, but he effortlessly made himself heard over the thump of the rock music shaking the floor beneath them.

Johann decided to yell. He cupped a hand over one ear as if he had trouble hearing the guy, but with his psi senses he could always tell. Voices articulated were always reflected in the mind and he could pick them up there. Telepathy was merely the spoken voice without the verbal aspect. "They have exams tomorrow. We're another band, so we decided to join up for tonight."

Hunter gave a sharp nod. "If you don't perform to my satisfaction I won't pay you and I'll make sure you don't get any more gigs in LA. You hear me?"

"Okay, man, I get your drift." God, could he sound any more sixties? That was why he avoided current slang. It dated too quickly. "We're good."

"You'd better be. So what's your name?"

Oh great, playing nice with future prey wasn't his idea of fun. "Kevin Smith," he said, using his cover mortal name. "I play guitar." He couldn't cross his fingers. He supposed he was telling a kind of truth, because he did take a couple of lessons once. Enough to know the guitar and he didn't make sweet music together. "We practiced with Andros and I think you'll like what we're going to do for you." Like hell they would. But he'd love the fuck out of it.

"You know what we are, what we do here?"

"Goth?" he offered. "Andros said something about vampires. Are there any here?"

Hunter smiled, revealing the glittering tips of his fangs. Johann gave him the wide-eyed awed look.

Let me read him.

Ah yes, Chase. He could pierce most shields, sometimes without detection. But not this time. The big guy put a hand to his head and shook it before he took a step back and turned to face his friends. "You do that?"

A red-haired vamp shook his head. "Do what?"

"Never mind." Goliath turned back to Johann, who'd decided to stay until the man dismissed him.

A movement on his other side distracted him. A female, a mortal from her mind-pattern, stepped forward with a swirl of enticing perfume and pure, feminine heat. In the old days she would have tempted him mightily, the old days being a couple of weeks ago, pre-Ania. From her high-piled gleaming black hair to the tips of her shiny patent thigh-boots she provided a treat for the eyes. Black and silver, but not in the profusion others wore it, and a painted sigil near her left eye. He liked that. This woman had come out in more ways than one, the tightly laced corset pushing her breasts up so they quivered with every breath. "I like this one. Better than the other guy. You want to play after you've—played?" She reached out and touched his cheek with one curved claw, long acrylic nails painted a shiny black, imitating a vampire's talons.

He repressed the reactive shiver she sent through his body. Anyone touching him with just that amount of pressure would evoke that.

"Ooo, baby." Without warning, she ran her hand down his body and grabbed his nuts through his jeans. He suppressed his urge to rip himself free and grab her, instead. Around her sweet neck. "Oh yes, I like." She glanced up at the big man. "Can I have him, Azreal?"

Azreal was born Frank Hunter, if he's the owner of this hole.

Chase's dry comment almost made Johann snort with unexpected laughter. But he kept his face and his outer mind clear.

Azreal-Frank took Johann's chin in his hand and turned his face gently to the light. "If you want, but, Sheila baby, when you're done, bring him back to me. I want to play with him."

"You could join us."

"No. You have your fun."

Sheila?

Johann pushed into her mind, keeping his touch gentle, only to find Chase there before him.

A bit crowded in here.

So leave.

He withdrew and concentrated on the other Talents.

Chase's voice sounded in the private channel, crisp and decisive, like a cool drink of water after a drought. *Okay, I'm contacting the agents outside and starting the countdown. We're going in five. Stay there until I join you. I want Sheila and Azreal available for questioning and the rest can go into a holding cell. The Talents go back to the cells at the Timothy. Can you handle it?*

They had three vampires and two shape-shifters from other teams assigned to them tonight. Between them they should manage to flash or transport most of the Talents, although the cells at the hotel were going to be a tad crowded by the time they'd done.

I want Andros out of here in three minutes. Okay?

Sure.

Be discreet.

Johann reached for Andros and locked his senses on to him. He needed to touch Andros to flash him out, but the psi contact ensured he wouldn't get away without him knowing. Andros stood at the far side of the club, talking to some girls. To some vampires, as a matter of fact. As Johann watched through Andros' eyes, the girl with him bared her fangs and smiled at him. Andros shuddered and Johann felt the ripple of sexual heat.

Shit. The boy wasn't far off an addict. Mortals could become addicted to the high vampires delivered when they fed. This one wanted it. He'd bet if he took his time he'd find others too. They'd come here for their high, feed the vamps and beg for it. A certain kind of vampire liked it too and it made for one sick relationship.

He'd never allow that to happen to him and Ania. Never. He'd have to feed from her rarely, pace them out or feed without injecting the endorphins into her. But he'd never, ever make her a blood addict.

Right then, right there, he knew he wouldn't say goodbye to her at the end of this assignment. One way or the other he wanted to be with her. They'd make it work. They had to.

Andros, we're out of here.

Ten minutes? A shocked pause followed and he knew why. Many mortals reacted like that to their first psi conversation. He was glad of it. It meant they hadn't tried to get into his head. Most likely Andros, as food, was no more than a sheep or a cow to them. Bastards.

No. Get here, now.

Another shocked silence before Andros murmured something to the women and began to move. Thank God he wouldn't have to go fetch him.

He sensed the kid's presence behind him, then the shock when Andros recognized Sheila. *This is the woman who fucked Ania over?*

Yeah. That's her. I don't recall seeing her here before.

Most likely she kept out of your sight. Pretend not to recognize her, if you can. We don't want her forewarned.

She looks so different. Yes, I can do that.

Sheila helped by stepping back so shadow covered her more completely. Johann felt a miasma descend over her and knew how she'd escaped Andros' attention. Someone, probably Hunter, had fuzzed her so Andros wouldn't notice her. Or she might have done it herself. All mortals had some extent of psi, but for the most part it remained inert. So if Sheila was protecting herself, or a mortal was doing that for her, that meant she'd been trained. And the people who understood how to do that best were either the IRDC or a known associate. Like Bennett.

Johann almost growled his satisfaction. They were so close now. He stepped back, closer to the rope barrier.

Andros cleared his throat. Johann wouldn't have heard the sound, but he sensed Andros' nervousness. "We-we need to get to the stage."

Johann remembered to glance at Azreal who nodded his permission. Geez he hated that guy. Just as well he was so well trained.

Isn't it? Chase's dry tones brought him back. *Get Andros back to his sister and then come back here. It'll have kicked off by the time you get back, so don't try to do anything fancy like flashing back to this spot.*

Landing in the same spot as another person would kill him and the person he materialized into. He knew better. They'd scouted a niche down the alley at the back of the club and he'd flash back there. Pity this place wasn't closer to the Timothy. Then he could run.

The guy did his unhooking and rehooking ritual with the rope and he stepped through, taking Andros' elbow to steer them back the way they came.

It wasn't until he'd steered the guy to the door at the back of the stage that he realized he hadn't shaken everyone off. One of the women Andros had been talking to had followed them.

He opened the door and tried to shut it in the vamp's face, but she pushed it wide and followed them through. It clanged to behind her. Johann turned to face her, urging Andros behind him. "Butt out, this guy is mine." For the first time that night he showed a little of his true nature, letting the tips of his fangs show before he retracted them.

"Oh no," she said, smiling. This one was a bleached blonde, dressed in the almost compulsory black, but without the chains and scarlet lipstick. She looked healthy. Probably from Andros' blood. "I've been working this boy for weeks. If he's anybody's he belongs to me."

"Not tonight," Andros said. "I'll come back, Greta, I promise. I owe this guy, okay?"

"You been taking something? I told you I wanted you clean and pure."

"No. Just a regular favor," Johann put in. "You don't look particularly hungry."

She licked her lips, the pink tongue sneaking out to swipe at the cherry red lips. She didn't need lipstick. Blood throbbed beneath her tongue. "But I might be hungry for something else. I've not seen you before, vampire." A frown creased her alabaster brow. "And I can't read your sigil. Are those fangs real?"

"Maybe you should have asked that before." Johann wondered if he could get rid of her without fuss, or whether he should just grab Andros and go. But she could raise the alarm and they didn't want that. "But yes, they're real. I need to feed. So how about I do that and then come back to see you?"

"Oh I don't think so. You're too much of a nuisance. I have a good thing going here and you're not gonna spoil it."

Johann whirled to face Hunter, who stood with his hands on his hips, grinning at them. Fucker was alpha to the max.

But then so was he. Two untrained vamps? Bring it on. He'd kill them both.

But before he could move, the guy placed one large hand on Andros' shoulder and flashed him out. Johann reached out, but too late, and whatever else he was, Hunter was tidy. No residue remained, not a trace to tell him where the bastard had taken Andros.

He had no choice. Johann turned around to face the female and spread his arms wide. "Take me to your leader," he said.

Chapter Fifteen

ಐ

Red seeped through his mind, his body and roared Johann back into consciousness. He bolted awake, but when he tried to sit up, he couldn't move. Bands covered his arms in two places, together with his legs and his waist. Groaning, he opened his eyes.

As he feared, he was alone. They'd restrained him with, he suspected, silver. But he was one of the Talents silver didn't affect. While silver allergy was high in the Talented community, it wasn't complete, although they'd allowed their enemies to think so. When the price of silver went up, they rejoiced because it added to the costs loaded on the IRDC and their ilk.

Bastards. He could break out of these restraints if he could access his vampire strength. But he couldn't. It must be daytime. Shit, that was a blow. But night or day he was still a trained agent and not without his own strengths.

He lay on a flat bed that was covered with something that rustled when he moved, probably plastic. A single sheet covered him, of the white starched hospital variety. A single light bulb hung overhead, seemingly designed to shine straight in his eyes. He glanced to one side and saw the inevitable large mirror, the two-way observation panel, presumably. When he turned his head he saw an array of surgical instruments laid out on a green cloth on a trolley. Since they were uncovered, his captors obviously meant them to intimidate. Johann decided to pick out the ones he'd go for first instead. Scalpels, hooks, even forceps would come in useful later. An oxygen tank rested against one wall but he doubted it was to do anything except bring him back if they went too far. He repressed a shudder of revulsion.

Andros. Oh fuck, Andros. Johann took a breath, then another one and only then tried to stretch his senses further than the room he lay in. No chance. He met a solid block. Since the silver thing didn't work for him, that left sonic interference. Telepathy seemed to work on frequencies, a bit like radio waves, and although they couldn't block all activity, putting up a sonic field to block ultra low and ultra high frequencies seemed to hamper most. It certainly hampered him.

Andros might not be in this building. He could be anywhere. Jesus, what a mess.

It wasn't in his nature to lie back and wait on events so he spent his time constructing various scenarios, what he'd do in certain situations. At least he had some kind of strategy ready. They wouldn't leave him alone for long. He was mortal, vulnerable. They could kill him easier in this state.

But if they'd wanted to do that, they'd have done it already. No, he was laid out like a specimen ready for experimentation. He'd seen and rescued enough of the IRDC's victims to know what that meant. They'd slice and dice him and leave him an hour before dawn so his body could effect some kind of healing.

Shit, waiting was hard.

He tried again, stretched out his senses—just as someone opened the door and shoved Andros into the room.

Bennett. Fuck and double fuck.

Andros looked far too pale for Johann's liking. He stumbled as he walked in but he didn't try to balance himself with his hands, because they'd fastened them together behind his back. He jerked his head, flicking his floppy fringe aside. Without the gel it drooped helplessly over his forehead. Without the eyeliner and cocky attitude he looked heartbreakingly young.

He stared at Johann and Johann forced a wry grin. "Sorry, kid."

"What for?"

"We promised to get you back before the raid started."

A man stepped into the room behind Bennett. Azreal. "Hello, Frank," Johann said.

Azreal still wore Goth-type clothes but he'd taken off his nipple clamps. Shame, Johann could have used them to cause him some serious damage. Perhaps that was the reason. He saw tiny red marks on either side of the guy's nipples, because naturally, he still wore the chain-encrusted vest and nothing underneath. Like some kind of torture master from the Middle Ages. His black leather pants molded to every crease of his body. Johann tried not to let his nostrils curl. He could almost smell the bastard from where he lay and he was still six feet away.

Bennett circled the table on which Johann lay. "We've met before."

"We have." A scent filled the air when Bennett walked up to his head, then reversed and walked the other way. Something he'd smelled before, but he couldn't think what it could be. Clinical, anesthetic, but more specific than that. He frowned when the starched white clinical coat flapped against the man's legs. He wore a thick pullover and jacket under it. Strange. This was LA, early spring. Few people here owned a pullover, much less wore it all day with a jacket over the top. Was he spending time in a freezer or was there another reason?

He remembered Bennett from before, his rotund figure usually covered by a conventional suit, a little the worse for wear. That was in New York, where at this time of year it was considerably colder than here in LA. He didn't go out, he kept the aircon high—and he'd lost weight.

Then he knew what he'd smelled under the smells of science. Sickness. Bennett was sick.

"I'm keeping you, you know that." The bastard sounded as clipped and precise as always. Frank smirked. "But I want someone else too. So you're helping me."

He leaned over and grabbed a scalpel from the tray. Before Johann could do anything, even cry out, Bennett swept it down his forearm, cutting a clean, deep slice. Blood poured from the wound.

Pain swamped Johann but he pushed it aside. No time for that now.

Frank lifted a small silver object. A camera? What the fuck?

Chapter Sixteen

80

Chase entered the room talking. "I'm stripping Sheila's mind. We need to get the information fast and we're running out of time."

Jillian, before then seated next to Ania, working on one of the laptops, leaped to her feet and flew to him, her hands gripping his arms as if she could keep him there by force. "No! I've seen what that does to you, I can't let you!"

Chase's expression softened when he turned his attention to her. "I promise to stop before that happens."

Jillian wasn't done. "You'll collapse."

Oblivious of the onlookers, Chase took her in his arms and gave her a fierce kiss. "No I won't, I swear it."

"Chase, no!"

"I have more to live for than I ever did. I swear I won't take any unnecessary risks."

"Not good enough." The previously self-contained Jillian burrowed into Chase's arms, clinging like a child.

"We need to find out whatever she knows and she's not telling. Time's running out and she's our only lead on where they're holding Johann. I have to do it."

Ania couldn't bear it any more, this waiting, and this time she might be able to help. "Let me see her before you try that. I know her. I might be able to do what you can't."

Chase stared, his blue eyes wide. She found it uncomfortable to meet that stare, but she held her ground.

She spread her hands. "What harm can it do?"

Chase sighed. "And you need to ask her some questions of your own, don't you? You need closure." She didn't bother to deny it. He probably read that in her mind. "Go then. Keep to the side of the room nearest the door and don't let her get between you and it. Do exactly as the guards tell you and when they say time is up you come out, no question. We don't have a lot of time."

She went before he could change his mind. She walked along the hallway of faceless, anonymous doors, turned left, walked along that one, turned left again and saw a door with two men on either side of it. Guards.

One nodded to her, a big man dressed in jeans and a tight-fitting black t-shirt. From the size of the muscles bulging over his chest and arms she guessed he might find it difficult to get something that didn't fit him tightly. The other, just as big but African-American, sporting a head of cornrows and braids that must have taken a day to produce, smiled tightly. "Hi. Chase told us you'd be coming. Don't let her get between you and the door. You have fifteen minutes and we'll be watching you all the time."

Before she could ask how, he opened the outer door. Another small area lay behind it, with a long two-way screen and another door. She took a moment to peer through the window.

The shock of black hair, shiny but messy, surprised her as soon as they let her into the cell. Sheila had always kept her hair smooth and fastened back. But not today. The remains of Gothic clothing that Sheila wore was another surprise. Dramatic, black, of course, a black silver-studded corset, over which her ample breasts swelled, and a pair of tight black pants. Her feet were bare. Maybe she'd had stilettos on and they'd taken them away.

Ania remembered the times she and Sheila had laughed together, times they'd worked themselves to exhaustion or gone out for a meal and just enjoyed each other's company. That was why Sheila's betrayal hit her so hard—she liked her.

Sheila had not only ruined her company, she'd violated Ania's trust, made her that much harder, that less willing to trust. Ania hated that more than almost anything else.

When she turned her head and stared at Ania, she knew she had to face her and ask her the one question she needed to know the answer to.

So she went in, aware that the guard behind her would stay and ensure her safety.

She faced her erstwhile friend and partner. "Why?"

Sheila smiled and leaned back in the hard chair that was all the furniture the room contained. "Immortality. Who wouldn't do anything for that?"

"Me." She didn't even have to think about her reply. It wasn't worth it, she would never swap her integrity for a lifetime of regrets. "Is that it? And why did you think Bennett could give that to you? What did he want in return?"

"He wants you. I don't know why." Sheila's mouth, still bearing remnants of heavy red lipstick, twisted in a sneer. "If I delivered, he'd give me what I wanted. He'd put me in a room with a vampire and let him convert me."

"Do you know how it's done?"

"Three bites and you're it." She slid down farther, then came to herself and straightened up, blinking. Her lashes were glued together by thick black mascara, making spiky clumps, her eyeliner had spread, giving her something a panda would envy. But her eyes flashed bright hatred at Ania.

It was Ania's turn to sneer. "You wrecked my business, lied to me consistently for years, cheated and stole from me, so I can't find it in my heart to be sorry for you. You're getting exactly what you deserve, bitch. They lied to you. It takes more than that to make a vampire. Otherwise, why isn't the world overrun with them?"

Sheila swallowed. "You're lying. I've seen it done."

"I don't owe you anything, least of all the truth, but they showed you what they knew you wanted to see. You've been

193

feeding them for nothing, Sheila. And serves you right." Sorrow filled her. She had trusted this woman.

Sheila lifted her hair off her neck. Ania worked hard not to react when she saw the ugly mark underneath, but the vampire had left his mark, two messy wounds barely scabbed over. "That was the third bite. Before tonight is over I'll be laughing at you."

"No you won't."

"Oh yes I will."

Ania turned to leave. She could do no more here. But before she reached the door she felt a stirring in the air, a change and she turned back to see Sheila's smile of triumph. "I can feel it. It's starting. Oh yes, I'd say it was worth it."

The door burst open and a hand reached through, grabbing Ania. She had no time to protest, no time to react before she was yanked out of the room. She twisted in her captor's arms to stare through the two-way mirror. Then she wished she hadn't because she'd never seen Sheila's head that shape, never seen her eyes bulge quite so much. Never heard a scream as bad.

Shock waves reached her, then they were through the outer door and the guard slammed his hand on a large button outside.

Silence. The guard released Ania and set her carefully on her feet. "Okay?"

She nodded and turned her head in the direction of a movement in the hallway. Chase, racing toward them. He came to a sudden halt. "Was that what I thought it was?"

The guard nodded. "I think so."

"If it was, it'll be over now. Release the lock." He touched Ania's shoulder and a shot of white heat went through her. While she was still recovering Chase nodded. "You're okay. They got you out in time." He glanced up. "Let me in."

They didn't argue. One of the men hit the button again and Chase went through. When Ania tried to follow, they held her back. She didn't fight free. Something was badly wrong, and fear chased around her body, making her tremble.

When Chase reappeared, he closed the door behind him. His mouth was set in a grim line. "She's dead."

"What?" The word tore out of her. "How could that happen?"

"They set a mental bomb in her. You must have triggered it somehow. We'll find out how later." He shook his head. "What did she say to you?"

"I saw," the larger of the two guards put in. "Some low-life vamp told her if they bit her three times, she'd make the change. My guess is it was something to do with that. Injecting more than endorphins with the third bite."

Chase sighed and ran his hand through his hair. It fell straight back into place, leaving him as immaculate as ever, but the expression on his face told a different story. "Jesus. When we get the law in place we can get whoever did it arrested for murder. But right now we can't prove it. We need those laws." He looked up. "Sorry."

A mix of emotions churned through Ania, but she knew she wasn't sorry. Not entirely. She felt regret that Sheila had fooled her, regret for all the customers they'd been forced to let down, regret that Sheila couldn't have lived long enough to tell them more. But all her fear, all her concern lay with Johann. If Sheila could have told them more, they might have gotten to Johann quicker. Her stomach tied itself in a knot just thinking about him. "What do we do now?"

"We work on getting Johann out."

At three p.m., the open laptop resting on Chase's desk pinged. Incoming mail, but this was a different chime. Chase leaped up from his place on the sofa next to Ania and raced to the laptop. He read the mail and then swore, a long string of curses so inventive Ania listened in amazement. She hadn't thought Chase capable. Old money upbringing and all, Chase was either inventive or knew some sleazy people. Then he swore in Spanish and Italian. But not Polish.

When he didn't say anything at once, her apprehension ratcheted up and her breath caught in her throat.

Jillian looked up from her own laptop. "What? What is it?"

Chase lifted his head and looked at them. Ricardo, Jack, Ania, Jillian and a couple of other STORM agents sat on the long sofas in Chase's suite, each with a laptop, each trying to use the data they had to track down the location of the Bennett labs.

Ania crossed the room and when Chase would have closed the laptop lid, she put her hand over his, restraining him. He froze, but he didn't force the issue because she'd already seen what he was trying to hide from her.

She stood stock still, stunned by what she saw.

Johann, fastened to what looked like an operating table by wide bands of a silvery-colored metal. Padlocks fastened the bands down. Johann's face was turned to the camera, his face stoically set but she saw how the tendons in his neck strained and guessed he'd set his jaw against showing pain.

Pain he must feel from the deep cut down the length of his forearm. Blood poured from the wound, down to the table and onto the floor.

Knowing she had little time before Chase recalled her, she tore her gaze away from the picture and touched the arrow on the keyboard with a shaking finger, to scroll the page down.

This was taken an hour ago. We've bound the wound up for now. We want Ania Zelinski, alone and unprotected. You have until an hour before nightfall. Then we'll drain him and take his Talent. Your choice.

Chapter Seventeen

ೞ

"Oh no!"

"Not the greeting a woman expects from her lover." Ania strolled into the little room, hands thrust in her pocket so he wouldn't see how much she was shaking.

"How did they get you?"

She swallowed back her tears. They were no doubt watching them, as a red light glowed on the camera mounted in one corner of the cell. At least they'd bound that horrific wound on his arm. "They exchanged me for Andros. It should have been you, but we thought they'd renege on that."

"Christ."

He looked far too pale for her liking. They must have let him bleed before they bound the wound. But he was alive and angry. She counted that a good sign because at least he had the energy to feel anger. They'd dressed him in a blue paper surgical gown, which in some ways was more humiliating than stripping him naked. The outfit reduced him to nothing, a cipher. Or tried to. Because the man lying on that table was anything but a cipher. Defiance delineated every hard muscle, every line of his lean face.

She switched to telepathy, reaching out for him deep down, on their private link. *Andros managed to say one word to me before he left. He said, "Cancer." And I think I know what he meant.*

Tell me. Here, his voice sounded calmer. And their link gave her shivers, even now when they were both in so much danger. She wanted him. She'd always want him.

Our mother died of leukemia. Andros and I were tested for bone marrow compatibility. We weren't compatible. But what if someone else got hold of those records?

Fuck, that's it!

A new light entered his eyes. Understanding, intelligence. *Bennett came to personally inflict the wound on me. He's lost a lot of weight and he looks pale. I smelled sickness on him. Shit, I think you've got it.*

Well, they let Andros go. I saw him get in the car with Chase. He'll tell them.

"Come here." A note of yearning entered his voice. She took the couple of steps that took her to the table and she smoothed her hand over his forehead. He felt cold. Far too cold for her liking. "They took a lot of blood to weaken me. Even when I turn vampire at sunset I won't be up to full strength. Not until I feed."

She stroked down his arms, wincing when she encountered the broad steel band that held him down. When she glanced away, he said, "No. Look later. First things first. Kiss me."

Yes, that was what she wanted too. Beyond all reason she wanted to kiss him. She bent and touched her lips to his and slowly increased the pressure until his mouth opened and she could slip her tongue inside.

It felt like coming home. His taste filled her mouth, addicting and every bit of it Johann. He groaned, sending vibrations resonating through her and instant arousal spiked her nipples, made her pussy dampen for him.

She drew away reluctantly and gazed deep into his eyes. "I love you."

His smile took them away from this bleak little room to a place of their own. "I love you too. When we get out of here we're going to do something about that."

His reference dragged her back to reality. "I'll look at these locks."

"You have a hairpin?" He huffed a cynical laugh. "I think it might take more than that."

I'm bugged and I let Chase in deep. He's not there now.

They'll have this place locked down. We can only communicate because we're in the same room. But he'll have tracked you as far as he can. I think we can safely assume they'll get here. Eventually.

Can we hold out?

She hated his hesitation. He didn't say a word, telepathically or otherwise. But she loved that he told her the truth with his next words. *I don't know.*

Devastation poured into her, filling that little spot of happiness he'd put there when he told her he loved her. "That means no, doesn't it?" She hadn't meant to speak out loud but telepathy still didn't come naturally to her and her default action was speech. Hearing it made it more real.

"You will. I might not." *They'll want to keep you alive long enough for you to donate the bone marrow to Bennett.*

His eyes gained a faraway look. He was thinking and he wasn't sharing his thoughts with her. That worried her. She straightened up and examined the fastenings holding him to the table. Clamped down hard, padlocks at each point. She'd have to undo each padlock separately. But when Johann turned vampire, he'd break through these bonds, no problem. So they would either move him or kill him before sundown. That gave them around three hours.

In three hours she might have lost the love of her life. Or her own life. Maybe she could strengthen him. *Feed from me. If he's going to take my marrow, then let me at least make you stronger.*

He opened his mouth and she felt the sound of *No* in her mind, but then he didn't say anything. He just stared at her.

"Yes," he said. "That's the thing. *Miláčku*, I can't take anything from you until nightfall. Sunset, to be precise."

The door behind her opened and she swung around, trying to protect Johann with her body. They wouldn't kill her, not yet anyway. But they might kill him.

A white-coated man wheeled in a trolley holding a series of covered humps. Ominous-looking covered lumps. He stopped short of Johann's table and leered at him. "Your favorite piece of furniture is back." Like a stage magician he whisked off the baby blue covering to reveal a display of surgical instruments and small bowls. She felt nothing from the man behind her, not a twitch, not a blink, but a carefully controlled lack of reaction.

"Not for you this time." He glanced at her. "For you."

When she lunged forward in a desperate attempt to grab something off the trolley he gave an easy laugh and moved it aside. "Don't. You'll only hurt yourself."

"And we can't have that, can we?"

She swung around to face the newcomer. Standing in the doorway, two burly minders behind him, stood a short, elderly man. No, he wasn't elderly, just middle aged. But his weary stance, the thin, wispy hair, his pale, papery skin, and the way the bones pushed against it, as if anxious to escape, all that made him look old.

Cancer will do that. And leukemia was one of the worst. Unless a bone marrow match could be found, and even then nothing was certain. The illness could be slowed down though. He wore a pair of gleaming gold-framed spectacles on the bridge of his nose, which jutted out, emphasizing the fine-drawn features of his face, the only live thing about him. Even his eyes looked sluggish and old, the eyelids hooded in creases over them.

"Mr. Bennett."

"Dr. Bennett," he corrected her. His voice was academically dry but it didn't sound as old as he looked. "And you're Ania Zelinski. A shame you have the same initial as your brother. I couldn't be sure which of you would provide what I need."

"Bone marrow."

He smiled. "Indeed. What a clever girl. Then your boyfriend here, or someone like him, will give me the other thing I need. Immortality."

"You'll have to get it somewhere else," Johann growled from behind her. "I can't give you immortality."

"Near enough for me. At least for now."

That was why Bennett was so desperate for fast results, why he'd left the relatively safe umbrella of the IRDC to strike out on his own. He was sick. The process of conversion took a toll on a healthy body. With someone as sick as Bennett looked, he wouldn't survive it.

But the news lightened his heart because it meant that they wouldn't kill him. Not just yet, anyway. He could have a chance. If Chase found them in time, if he could keep Ania alive, if he got that one opportunity to break free…

Not too many "ifs". He could do this. He had to. They couldn't leave him bound here after sunset, they'd have to move him or he'd break out of here too fast for them. This was a typical IRDC-style lab and he'd liberated enough of those to know what they'd do. They'd put silver into the mix, they'd have chains and restraints strong enough to hold him, but they might have someone else there. Another vampire or a shape-shifter. Insurance. Or an alternative.

Shit, he'd have to take his chances when they happened. He couldn't afford to wait, not with Ania in danger. He'd die for her, he knew that without even pausing to consider it, but he wouldn't watch her die.

Bennett watched him with a kind of sick satisfaction. "I need a sample of her bone marrow so I can confirm it's what I want. You know that." And he knew that Bennett wouldn't want him leaving this place alive. Feed the man's oversize ego, that might work.

"You can have me. I'll convert you without a struggle if you let her go."

"I need her."

"I know you do. But you don't have to kill her." He kept his voice steady and reasonable. He should plead, but he couldn't do it. Couldn't beg this man who took masochistic pleasure in tormenting people.

Bennett leaned over to the table and picked up a large syringe with a hollow needle.

He grinned at Johann. "Behave yourself, lie there and don't fight and I'll give her anesthetic before I aspirate."

If he didn't use anesthetic it would hurt like hell, near to killing her. Jesus, he wouldn't do that. Fear swept across him, fear for Ania, not for himself.

"What do you want?" He ripped the words out, unwilling to concede anything. He'd tear this man apart given half a chance.

"I want you to lie still while they take those bands off you and replace them with something stronger. We're going to need them come sunset, aren't we? We need to make you a bit more secure. You lie there and let them bind you and I'll administer anesthetic before I aspirate her."

"Deal."

Bennett picked up a smaller syringe and stuck it in Ania's arm. He wasn't particularly careful, but it wouldn't hurt like the big one would. Still, Johann promised the bastard would pay for every twinge he caused her.

The clanking, straight out of a medieval torture chamber, told him they had the damn restraints ready.

Three men entered, dragging heavy chains and holding handcuffs of a slim material Johann suspected was something high-tech and unbreakable. From medieval to modern, they were taking no chances. Bands to hold a man wouldn't hold a vampire, even one depleted from lack of blood. He guessed they'd drained him of two or three pints, something it would take him a few hours to make up as a vampire if they brought him food. He knew what they'd do. After sunset they'd drain him completely, force him into the blood-madness that would make him take and take anybody that came near enough for him. He wouldn't stop, not until he'd taken it all, and then blood-fever would affect the subject and he'd turn.

Bennett wanted to be that man, the subject, the born-again vampire. Johann had already thought about that and he had one way out that would save Ania and destroy Bennett.

"Bone marrow therapy is often used in conjunction with other treatment, like chemotherapy and interferon, but I don't need that." Bennett held the needle high in the air so it caught the light. The fucking thing glinted wickedly and he felt Ania shudder. "I just need to be strong enough to withstand the conversion. I don't need anything else. I've had chemo and the premeds. I can do this tonight if I need to. I'm ready."

He was so fucking confident he wasn't even hiding what he wanted. He'd move them, or he'd plan to, something Johann was sure of when his minions made him sit so they could fasten his hands together behind his back. Then they lashed his ankles together. The bastards cinched his wrists so hard they all but cut off the circulation. Not that Bennett would care if he had hands or not. They fastened his arms at the upper shoulders, then they wrapped the chains around his ankles and he realized they weren't to restrain him, they were meant to hobble him. They weighed a ton, or they felt as if they did.

Bennett prodded a now sleepy Ania toward the table Johann had just vacated. She went without protest and lay down. Johann watched, knowing that this time at least, Bennett wouldn't kill her. Not until he was sure he had enough marrow to strengthen himself. Johann calculated rapidly and realized Bennett wouldn't need long. If he was on the edge, he'd know precisely when he could take the conversion. Then time would be up.

Bennett glanced up at Johann. "When I've done this procedure, we're moving to a high security facility."

"It won't help you." He couldn't bear to witness what the bastard was doing to Ania, but he couldn't look away. The doctor pulled down her pants and panties and swabbed the area he wanted to aspirate. Johann had thought the arm maybe or the thigh, but no, the fucker was going for her hip. The minions, still in the room, stared at Ania's soft white skin avidly. Bennett wouldn't let them touch her, not until he had what he wanted. That was the only thing that held him back, that stopped him straining against his bonds until he died or broke out of them. She was his and nobody hurt what Johann had vowed to protect.

* * * * *

Clouds obscured her vision. She was lying in a field, lush green grass cushioning her. The sun dazzled her eyes and she couldn't see but she didn't care. He'd take care of her. But her chest hurt. She lifted her hand to rub at it and heard Johann's voice. "Try not to do that, *miláčku.*"

She opened her eyes and squinted against the dazzling light. Only then did the memories return to her in a flood. She wanted the field back.

When she turned her head to avoid the light, she saw Johann, now lashed to a chair with gleaming, slender bands of something that looked nastily high-tech and unbreakable.

He'd turned vampire. She rolled over to face him and winced. Her hip hurt. "What did they do?"

"They took marrow, but only a sample. They want to test it for suitability, but they'll be back for more. They'll keep you alive so they can harvest you as needed." The bleak light made the sharp features of his face even more pronounced. His tan pale now, his face haggard, she wanted to comfort him even more than she wanted to recover from the debilitating pain and blood loss she'd suffered. "They haven't fastened you down, *miláčku.* See if you can move."

Cautiously she stretched her legs. Her hip hurt, and she certainly felt the aftereffects of the anesthetic, plus the blood loss from the procedure but she was far from finished. She swung her legs over the side of the table and sat up, allowing herself a few seconds for the inevitable dizziness to subside. She braced her arms on the table, the creased cloth under her palms giving her the sense of reality she needed to bring herself around. They didn't have much time, she didn't need Johann to tell her that. They'd be back.

She lifted her head and stared at her lover. If she couldn't get him out of the metal bands, she sure as hell couldn't get him out of the slimmer, but thicker bands that bound him now.

He smiled and it looked incongruous and completely right. Because he was only looking at her. "Come over here and kiss me."

Whatever else was wrong, this was most definitely right. She got to her feet, steadied herself on the table and crossed the room to where Johann sat on the chair. He looked up at her, smiling.

"You've turned vampire. It must be after sundown."

"So it is." His smile held all the feral joy of his being. "Sit on my lap and kiss me. I'll think better if you do that."

She couldn't resist his allure, the warmth and tinge of danger she felt in his embrace. Not that he could embrace her now but at least she could touch him, kiss him. Sitting down, she felt secure, safe, everything she shouldn't feel now. But when she touched her lips to his, she felt more and when his tongue invaded her mouth, taking control even though he was the one tied up, a curl of pure sexual excitement wove its way through her body.

His mouth left hers to nip and kiss her cheek, then lower, until he reached her neck. She almost didn't recognize the sting as his fangs touched her sensitive skin, then she shuddered.

He pulled away, and smiled up at her, the tips of his fangs gleaming wickedly as he withdrew them. "I don't care who's watching. I want you."

She glanced up at the camera behind them. "I want you too." They'd put her in a pale blue surgical gown like the one he wore so it took very little for her to lift it and dispose of the paper panties underneath. He wore nothing under his, she could see the bead of liquid staining the thin fabric above where his cock strained toward her. She eased back in his lap and drew up the single layer that separated them. She loved his cock, pulsing long and hard just for her.

"Are you ready for me, my love?"

She had a moment of doubt. "What are we doing?"

"Don't think. Give us this moment of respite. The pause before the second battle. Let's celebrate just being alive and with each other."

She couldn't resist. Rising up, she grasped his shaft, loving the sheer strength of him. Soft skin to protect her from the rigidity beneath. Hardness to breach her giving pliability. A perfect match. She rose up and poised over the tip, watching as she pushed down and forced him inside.

He parted her swollen flesh, opening her with his first, deep thrust. Although his arms and legs were bound and his waist fastened to the chair, his lower body still had a little movement. Enough to plunge into the depths of her body.

She watched as he entered and retreated, could just see his wet, red shaft move below the open vee of her pussy, decorated with the glistening little nub that was her clit. Like this, he touched her every time he drove in and it added a thrill each time, to add to the sensations he brought to her deep inside. He sat up and the contact grew firmer.

"Come down here," he murmured. "Let me kiss you."

She curved her hand around his neck and kissed him. Madness, to be fucking in the midst of danger but she needed love and reassurance and maybe he did too. For whatever reason this felt right.

Their lips met and while he kept up the rhythm, their kiss added sweet spice to the encounter. When she opened her mind to him he surged in, filling her as he'd never done before, holding her to him with his mind and body. She reveled in the tight grip he had on her, never wanted him to set her free because at this moment she felt freer than at any time in her life.

His lips traveled across her cheek, down her neck to the little pulse at the base of her throat. When she felt the prick of his fangs there she rejoiced.

The sharp twin pain as he entered was no more than a twinge, soon over, then the sense of having him in her, drinking her, swept over her. She'd lost blood, but he'd lost a lot more. He needed this. He drew, harder than he had before. Only when she realized there was more than sexual intent to this did a touch of cold fear edge her sexual heat.

"Johann…"

Relax.

She touched his head, wove her fingers into his hair, held him close. "Take what you need."

Her toes felt cold. Hardly unexpected, since they'd taken her clothes away and she only had the same kind of surgical gown Johann wore.

His lovemaking eased so she increased her movements over him until he was hardly moving and she was doing all the work. She didn't care. It felt as good and this way she could direct the plunges. But strange aches and pains began to trouble her. A twinge in her back, and she could hardly feel her feet now. "Johann…"

Ania, I love you so much, and this is the only way I can think of saving you. Let me do this.

What, what are you doing?

They plan to kill you. They'll take all your marrow, not just the little they need. When you were unconscious they taunted me. I can't get free of these bonds, I can't save you like this. But if I give you my Talent, your metabolism will change and so will the nature of your blood. It won't be compatible with Bennett's. And you're free. You can get out of here. Without my strength they'll kill us both. Long before the cavalry gets here.

"No!" With a sharp tug she tried to pull away but she couldn't. He held her tight, despite his bonds. She was too weak now. If she got free she'd probably bleed to death, and from the strength of the suction on her neck, that wouldn't take long.

And then she'd take from him, she'd kill him.

The door burst open. Bennett. She might have known he'd stop them. Hands around her waist, intrusive, hateful hands tried to drag her off him, but Johann held her firm.

Then a voice, the last voice she expected to hear. "Let her go, Johann." And a mind, steel-sharp, sliced between them, severing the connection. She fell back, crushing Chase under her until he turned with a practiced movement and rolled her under him.

He got to his feet. He held a fine saw in his hand, one of those power tools surgeons used to drill into skulls. None of this made sense.

Black edged her vision but from her position on the floor she saw Jack dragging a huge figure across the threshold. And behind him Ricardo, half-shifted, held his arms tight to his sides.

Azreal. This guy was a vampire and if Johann was in control of his powers, so was Azreal. How could they hold him?

When Jack glanced at her she saw how. Jack didn't seem as at ease with his other half, his shape-shifted form but for this he'd gone feral. His eyes were cats' eyes, glowing gold in a face with a flatter nose, a pointed chin. His skin seemed to have patches, markings, but she couldn't be sure because her vision had dimmed so she seemed to have heavy black gauze between her and the rest of the world.

Ricardo gave Azreal a sharp shove, driving him to his knees. His chain belt clanked when it hit the floor. She watched, detached now, their voices empty echoes in her head. And all the time Johann called to her.

Then even that stopped and a warm mouth settled on her skin, fangs coming down to taste her blood.

Chapter Eighteen

ജ

"Bastards! She'll die!"

"No she won't. He will." Chase strode behind him and used the little drill. He couldn't see what he was doing but first one bond loosened, then the other.

By this time Azreal lay on the floor next to Ania, sucking at the wound Johann had made. It was almost unbearably intimate, but Johann set his teeth and realized what Chase was doing. "You're using Compulsion."

"You want to report me for illegal activity?"

His bonds free, Johann brought his wrists forward and rubbed them hard. "Are you fucking kidding? Maybe I'll report you for a medal. They were going to kill her. I had twenty minutes before they were coming back, but I didn't tell her that. What was I supposed to do?"

"So you thought you'd die for her?" Jack made a sound of derision.

"They had me tied up tight. What did you use to free me?"

Chase buzzed the saw before his face. "High-tech thing made for surgical uses. I replaced the skull borer with a saw meant for artificial joints. I've got to get me one of these. I like it." He grinned and buzzed the instrument again before he dropped it into his pocket.

Johann stood and covered what was left of his erection, which wasn't much. When she'd tumbled back, the gown had fallen over Ania's pussy, something he could only be glad of. Or he might have killed someone, especially that bastard now greedily drawing up what was left of her blood.

He extended his senses and found her mind faltering, wandering. She didn't really know what was going on anymore. A blessing, he thought. But he held her, protected her. Until Chase intervened.

Johann hadn't noticed Chase's grip on his arm but he did see the steel shutter in his mind because he sure as fuck hadn't put it there.

His fangs came down and he growled low.

"Don't go there, Johann. The madness will come on her. If you're linked with her, you'll get it too."

Shit, the fucker was right. Emotions tore through him at hurricane force, leaving him just as battered as if he'd stood in the path of a tornado. He wanted—needed to protect her but if he entered her mind again now, they'd both be in a shitload of trouble.

All he could do was watch. Something he wasn't very good at. The bastard was making a meal of Ania. He watched the color leech from her skin.

He watched her die.

Azreal tried to cheat, tried to pull back just before the last, choking breath that signified her death, but Chase held him there. Sweat broke out on Chase's face, dripped from his chin on to his gray t-shirt and dark utility vest.

And Azreal slumped back to suck the last drops of blood from Ania.

Her eyes stared blankly up at nothing. That body, those beautiful eyes seemed just like any other with the life gone from them.

A pulse in her neck throbbed, just once, and Azreal cried out. Johann had never heard fear so eloquently expressed before. He leaned on the back of the chair where he'd been confined, unwilling to reveal how weak he still was despite the ingestion of Ania's precious blood. It would be coursing around his system now, revitalizing every part of him. He wanted to give it back to her.

Then an unholy growl sounded low in every corner of the room. Ania's eyes flashed red and black pooled over them, leaving none of the heavenly blue. They glistened with intent and she rolled, pushing Azreal to the floor.

Fangs burst down out of her mouth, slicing her lower lip. Vampires learned to tuck the lip away when their fangs descended. Hers would heal soon enough if this worked. If. Terror pulsed through Johann. He couldn't live without her. He lifted his gaze and met Jack's solemn expression before he recalled that Jack's love, the jaguar shape-shifter Carilla Vargas, had barely converted him before she was killed. Bennett had to pay for that crime too. He prayed they had the fucker locked down tight this time. Then he could tear his throat out and let Jack maul what was left. They both owed him.

Ania was beyond anyone's control now. At the time of her death she drew a precious hormone from Azreal, something a vampire only released at his impending death. They'd kept this secret for generations and would keep it forever as far as Johann was concerned. If anyone like Bennett got to know about it, they'd treat vampires like farm animals.

It was unusual for any non-vampire to witness a conversion. To keep the secret, they'd always treated it as a ritual and banned non-vamps from taking part, but it couldn't be helped this time. No way would he ask his friends to leave. So Jack, Chase and Ricardo watched as Ania drew the lifeblood out of Azreal.

The extra blood would give her strength to survive the change. Over the next few weeks her organs would adapt, change and grow to take account of her new state. That was why vampire society was convinced vampires and mortals had the same ancestry, why they were all humans of some sort. They could breed, they could convert, so it stood to reason. Not that Johann had taken much interest before. Now as he watched the life flood back into Ania's body, he could only be glad of it.

This process would exhaust her. She was drawing the blood up the hollow fangs and it went to the organ that did nothing as far as mortals were concerned. Except that hormone rushed it into life. Situated near the kidneys, the organ did its work by transforming the blood, much as the lungs converted air or the stomach converted food, all to energy and vital forces the vampire needed.

He had little to do except watch and guard her for the next twenty minutes. The occasional crash and yell outside the now open door meant little to him. Nothing mattered outside this room.

Azreal stared into space. He must know his end had come. Johann tried to imagine how that would feel and knew that if he were lying there letting Ania take his life's blood, he'd be rejoicing. Because she would live. His original idea was to give her his Talent and then she'd be able to break out and escape. They wouldn't know she was vampire, they wouldn't expect an attack from her. Weakened from the operation, out of her depth in his world of Talents and spies, they'd discounted her. Wouldn't expect it from her. She'd get away, he knew it.

But now, this unexpected twist had given him pause. What would they do now? He loved her and she said she loved him but that was when she'd thought he was dying. He'd accepted what she said like a man dying of thirst in the desert would take water, without question and as the best thing he'd ever heard in his life, but now he had to give her a chance, let her make the decision once she was awake and in control.

But not yet. She'd need someone to look after her.

And he needed to know what was going on. "How did you find us so fast?"

Chase grinned. "The electronic bugs lasted longer than the mental trace. They cut that off soon enough, knocked her unconscious, but we planted bugs everywhere. They didn't strip her until they had her here."

"Bennett's slipping. He'd never have allowed that before. He's not thinking straight. You know he has leukemia?"

All three men tore their attention away from Ania to stare at him. "You're shitting me!" Ricardo said, but a smile curled at the corner of his mouth. "Could it be there's something to divine retribution?"

"We can only hope." Chase folded his arms and took the mental leap. "So Ania was a match?"

"Their mother had leukemia, so Ania and Andros were both tested. They weren't compatible but their results went into the system. Bennett must have picked them up from there. He came to LA specifically for them."

"So why did he try to kill them at Ania's apartment?"

Jack raised a brow. "We still don't know it was Bennett's people. The IRDC is still out there."

Understanding dawned on Johann. "Shit, yes. And their agents want to stop Bennett as much as we do. Even if it means killing his saviors. If they discovered Ania and Andros were possible marrow matches, they wouldn't hesitate."

Chase grunted. "They don't have the same scruples that we do about killing innocent people. I'll try to confirm it."

Johann grinned. He could afford to grin now that Ania was going to live. "I didn't think to scan their minds while they were firebombing Ania's apartment." His good humor faded. "She's lost her personal possessions, lost her business, lost who she is. I have a lot to make up to her and I intend to do it. If necessary STORM will have to take second place."

A brief silence before Jack spoke. "Wow. You really do have it bad."

Johann decided not to say anything. He settled back to watch his woman feed.

Chapter Nineteen

ಐ

"Where do you think you're going?"

Ania turned around from the mirror to see the much more appealing sight of Johann entering the bedroom. "Andros has his last exam today. I wanted to wish him luck."

Johann held out a cell phone. "Use this."

"I wanted to catch him at college before he went in. I haven't been around much recently."

He strolled up and put the phone on the vanity in front of her. Since he was leaning forward anyway, he touched his lips to her neck. "You've been busy."

She laughed and leaned back into his hold. "With you and Ricardo."

He straightened up and met her gaze in the mirror. "He's gone."

"Ricardo?" Startled, she turned around. He folded her in his arms and immediately she felt that sense of belonging that astonished her every time she felt it. She'd been lost so long before she found him.

"Ann Reynolds called from STORM. She doesn't want us to hunt for Bennett anymore. He keeps getting away, obviously has his escape routes well planned. So we're to follow the money instead. The IRDC has shared the information with us, after some not-so-gentle persuasion from Ricardo's brother Sandro. So we're going away soon."

Anxiety tightened her throat. "Where?" So she wasn't so safe after all.

"Following the money. You'll be with me."

She lifted her head to meet his eyes. She loved them, dark, soft and velvety. She'd better make the most of them. "You must know I can't."

He dropped a kiss on her brow. "Not for a couple of weeks, I know. You want to keep Andros company while he finishes his exams, but if you want to see him after that, you'd better stick with me, baby." He finished the sentence in a Bogart-like drawl, but she didn't smile.

She lifted her hand to cradle his cheek. "Andros' still ill. He still needs me. I have to stay here."

"You didn't hear me. Andros just accepted a job with STORM."

"Oh no!" Not Andros, not in that kind of danger. He was mortal, fragile from an illness he did his best to ignore. He'd be dead in a year.

"Not as an agent, *miláčku*. Andros is to join one of the teams as a researcher."

"Like Jack?" She remembered Jack as she'd seen him in Bennett's lab, with his cats' eyes gleaming from a leanly handsome human face, danger limned in every contour of his lithe body.

"No, not like Jack. Jack chose to move from researcher to agent. Most researchers stay in the office, safely tucked away with their computers and books. The team contacts them. That's what Andros will do. At a very good salary, I might add. He'll be fine, Ania."

Tension tightened her stomach, but she forced it down. Andros had to live his own life, whatever that would turn out to be. "They'll look after him, won't they?"

"We have very good medical facilities. And he can go on the list for conversions. Andros' in the best place to take advantage of that." He paused. "There's something else. Bennett and his cohorts know you're not a match for him anymore, not since you turned vampire. Your blood changes when you turn. But we have no way of knowing if Andros is a match too and until then he's better with us than outside."

She might have guessed that Johann would pick up on her tension and try to reassure her. And he was right. His hold on her tightened. "Your life is my life now. Never forget that."

"As if you'd let me!" She forced a smile and looked up at him. Then she didn't have to force it anymore. Just looking at him was enough sometimes. She couldn't believe he loved her, but since he told her several times a day she had to. And she knew she loved him. Unable to resist she stood on tiptoe to capture his mouth in a kiss.

His lips moved over hers, opened but he didn't try to take over. He let her kiss him and it was one of the sweetest things she'd ever felt. To have this frighteningly strong man under her control gave her such a strong sense of power she was almost afraid of it.

Or would be if she didn't love him so much. His hands came up to clasp her forearms, to urge her closer. His erection burgeoned against her stomach and she wriggled and opened her mind so he could see the heat he evoked in her.

He wrenched his mouth away. "You can't want this. You're still recovering."

"I want it. I want you." He pulled away and she grew frantic, panic coloring her words. "Johann, please. You've been so fucking gentle. I don't want gentle anymore. I'll learn to feed, learn to do all the things I have to, but with you. Can we just do something I know how to do?"

He gazed down at her and sighed, the soft groan emerging with the outbreath. "Do you know how hard it's been? But you were exhausted, my love. You needed the rest."

"Making love isn't something I count as work."

He laughed. "I guess I was somewhat overprotective. But I've never had anyone of my own before, someone to care for as I care for you."

"Never?"

He shook his head. "But you—you turn me inside out."

She leaned toward him and this time he didn't back off, only responded when she touched his lips with hers. That happened a bare second before he banded his arms around her and lifted her off her feet. He walked to the bed and tossed her on to it, but he gave her no time to do more than gasp a laugh before he landed over her. Even then he was careful to keep his weight off her, supporting himself on his elbows. She laughed into his mouth when he kissed her. Then she didn't laugh anymore.

He stripped the t-shirt over her head in one swift move, returning to her bra to free her breasts in record time. He pushed up and gave himself a moment to stare down at her.

She felt uncomfortable at first, remnants of a lifelong reticence and her lack of experience, but then she heated. He just looked, watched as her nipples crinkled into tight points under his regard, and when he spoke his voice was deep and lust-drenched. "I've never, ever seen anything as beautiful. Anything as fucking aphrodisiac as that. Just you, Ania."

With a groan of surrender he descended and took one taut tip into his mouth. She gave a sharp cry and arched up to him as pure sensation radiated from her nipple through to her whole body, sending it into tingling alert.

Then he touched her clit, fingered it and pinched it between his finger and thumb. He hadn't touched her for days and now he was all over her, stroking, pinching, sucking. He lifted his head, his eyes glowing even though it was still daylight. "I'm ravenous for you, Ania. I'm taking you now, making you mine. You hear?"

She nodded, bit her lip. "I was always yours."

He slid his hand around her thigh, touched her anus and circled it, something he was well aware drove her crazy. How had she never discovered it before Ricardo and Johann came into her life? It was like her sex life had been incomplete before them and most especially Johann. He knew what she wanted, not only because he could read her desires but because he could read her body as well as her mind. And right now her pussy was showing him in the best way, soaking the sheet below them, her eagerness to have him inside her transmitting itself to every part of her muscle-tensed body.

He kissed her, lifted her breast to reach the tender underside, took his time circling and loving her navel before he kissed farther down and hovered over her pussy.

She grabbed his thigh, tugging until he got the message and slid around so that when he took possession of her clit with his mouth, she had his cock within reach. Within reach of her mouth. She could give him some of the exquisite torture he was subjecting her to.

And he tasted good. When she swiped her tongue over the glistening head her moan equaled his. Of course, he was by now licking her out, enjoying the feast as if he hadn't eaten for days. In a way, he hadn't. Neither had she.

So she enjoyed him now, touched her tongue to the tiny opening and explored it, the musky, salty taste she craved. If she could get addicted, this would be it, the fresh liquid seeping from the tip of his cock.

She lapped it up as he gave it to her, pushing into her mouth until he hit the back of her throat. She couldn't take him farther, he was too big, but perhaps another time, when she lay in a better position, perhaps with her head tipped farther back, she'd sure like to try. The thought of taking him in completely made her want it, but she couldn't do it now. So she settled for working her mouth over him, tightening her jaws until she could suck hard, trying to draw everything out of him.

But he distracted her by licking her out, slurping as he got nearer to her pussy. *You are so wet and I want it all. Every bit is mine.*

The words stroked her mind as he was stroking her body, taking her heart with his body, his mind. And giving her himself in return.

He drank her in and she wished he'd give her what he had in return. She cupped his balls, pulled the loose skin tight over them and heard his responsive groan. She needed it like she needed to breathe.

And then the new sensation swept over her and she knew the sun had dipped below the horizon. She turned vampire. Warmth filled her and she felt the toothbuds, dormant during the day, gain a tenderness that meant her fangs could emerge. Strength coursed through her body, power adding to her raging libido.

But the man making love to her was as strong as she was. Stronger. And she was still learning to control the strength, the new power, so fearful she might hurt him, she began to pull away and regretfully let his hot, hard cock slip from her mouth.

Johann tightened his hold on her and pulled her back so she sucked him in again. She couldn't resist. She licked the ridge under the cock head and tasted it, suckled it.

"Baby, bite me."

She couldn't believe it. Perhaps she'd misheard.

You heard right. Bite me. I've always wanted a woman to do that for me. You know how to heal the wounds afterward, you won't hurt me. Much. His whole body shuddered in a convulsive wave that seemed to travel from his toes up. *Please.*

As a new vampire, she needed to feed almost daily and Johann had been careful to ensure she did. From him. Eventually she'd go out and find her own prey. They'd feed together, he promised her. But she'd fed from his neck or his wrist, or one memorable time, from his chest. Not this.

Her fangs emerged as she thought about it and she realized how much the thought turned her on. Or maybe it was his desire, she couldn't say which and right now it didn't seem to matter much.

For the first time she felt full vampire hunger and realized he'd been in her mind before, tempering her hunger. But now he hadn't done it and the full force of hunger roared through her. She wanted him in every way.

She didn't have to do much to sink her fangs into his cock. Only let it happen. She was afraid, of course she was, but he wanted this and so did she. If she backed off now it would only be her fear controlling her and she wouldn't allow that.

As the razor-sharp tips sank into the delicate flesh she felt a sting in her labia and her need, which she'd thought at the very summit, soared up even more. He was tasting her. For the first time in her vampire existence her lover fed off her.

They connected, love and trust combining to bind them more than any formal ceremony, any other form of pact and she knew what he'd been telling her was right. They were together. They belonged together, linked as they were now.

Ania had no way of knowing how long it took but she trusted Johann to stop her, although she wondered what it would be like to take all of his life-essence while he was taking hers.

And when she came it was like nothing she'd ever known before. She screamed, letting all of her passion out, mindlessness holding her captive, everything freezing except pure sensation. His cries mingled with hers and she swallowed what he gave her, savoring the taste of the man she loved.

When he drew back she felt the soft touch of his tongue, healing the small punctures he'd made. She did the same when he guided her to do so, putting an unspoken request in her mind.

And then she lay on her back while he came up the bed and guided himself inside her. Only when he'd joined them and she'd curled her legs around his waist did he speak again. "All my life was only leading up to this—my time with you." He cupped her cheek in one hand, as tender as he'd been passionate a moment before. "You have me, Ania."

"As you have me."

He pushed and she felt him, hard and ready again, push deep inside her and touch her sweet spot with every stroke, the way only he knew how to do. "Then marry me."

About the Author

෨

Lynne Connolly writes for a number of online publishers. She writes paranormal romance, contemporary romance and historical romance. She is the winner of two Eppies (now retitled the EPIC ebook awards) and a goodly number of Recommended Reads etc from review sites.

While these are very gratifying, that isn't why she writes. She wants to bring the stories in her head to life and share them with others, in the hope that they might give her some peace.

She lives in the UK with her family, cat and doll's houses. Creating worlds on paper or in miniature seems to be her specialty!

෨

The author welcomes comments from readers. You can find her website and email address on her author bio page at www.ellorascave.com.

Tell Us What You Think

We appreciate hearing reader opinions about our books. You can email us at Comments@EllorasCave.com.

Why an electronic book?

We live in the Information Age—an exciting time in the history of human civilization, in which technology rules supreme and continues to progress in leaps and bounds every minute of every day. For a multitude of reasons, more and more avid literary fans are opting to purchase e-books instead of paper books. The question from those not yet initiated into the world of electronic reading is simply: *Why?*

1. *Price.* An electronic title at Ellora's Cave Publishing runs anywhere from 40% to 75% less than the cover price of the exact same title in paperback format. Why? Basic mathematics and cost. It is less expensive to publish an e-book (no paper and printing, no warehousing and shipping) than it is to publish a paperback, so the savings are passed along to the consumer.

2. *Space.* Running out of room in your house for your books? That is one worry you will never have with electronic books. For a low one-time cost, you can purchase a handheld device specifically designed for e-reading. Many e-readers have large, convenient screens for viewing. Better yet, hundreds of titles can be stored within your new library—on a single microchip. There are a variety of e-readers from different manufacturers. You can also read e-books on your PC or laptop computer. (Please note that Ellora's Cave does not endorse any specific brands.

You can check our website at www.ellorascave.com for information we make available to new consumers.)

3. *Mobility.* Because your new e-library consists of only a microchip within a small, easily transportable e-reader, your entire cache of books can be taken with you wherever you go.

4. *Personal Viewing Preferences.* Are the words you are currently reading too small? Too large? Too... ANNOYING? Paperback books cannot be modified according to personal preferences, but e-books can.

5. *Instant Gratification.* Is it the middle of the night and all the bookstores near you are closed? Are you tired of waiting days, sometimes weeks, for bookstores to ship the novels you bought? Ellora's Cave Publishing sells instantaneous downloads twenty-four hours a day, seven days a week, every day of the year. Our webstore is never closed. Our e-book delivery system is 100% automated, meaning your order is filled as soon as you pay for it.

Those are a few of the top reasons why electronic books are replacing paperbacks for many avid readers.

As always, Ellora's Cave welcomes your questions and comments. We invite you to email us at Comments@ellorascave.com or write to us directly at Ellora's Cave Publishing Inc., 1056 Home Avenue, Akron, OH 44310-3502.

ELLORA'S CAVE

Romanticon

Annual convention
for women who
refuse to behave

WWW.JASMINEJADE.COM/ROMANTICON
For additional info contact: conventions@ellorascave.com

Discover for yourself why readers can't get enough
of the multiple award-winning publisher
Ellora's Cave.

Whether you prefer e-books or paperbacks,

be sure to visit EC on the web at
www.ellorascave.com

for an erotic reading experience that will leave you
breathless.